PHOTOGENIC

A NOVEL BY

CHERYL MITCHELL WADE

This is a work of fiction. It is not meant to depict, portray, or represent any particular gender, real persons, or group of people.

All the characters and dialogues are products of the author's imagination and are not to be construed as real.

Copyright ©2015 Cheryl Mitchell Wade
ISBN 9780692175316

Edited by:
Karl Klausner

Cover and Book Design:
Mario Zelaya, Zelaya Designs, Santa Rosa CA

This book is dedicated with love

To my son

Carison Aaron Wade

To my parents

Ralph Brewer Mitchell and Dolores Mitchell

"I Know Where I'm Going and I Know the Truth.

I Don't Have to be What You Want me to be.

I'm Free to be What I Want"

--- Muhammad Ali

"Go confidently in the direction of your Dreams!

Live the Life You've imagined"

--- Henry David Thoreau

C O N T E N T S

PHOTOGENIC

A NOVEL BY

CHERYL MITCHELL WADE

CHAPTER 1

GETTING TO KNOW THE GRANTS

✦

My name is Gisele Grant and I'm more than happy to share this story about the three generations of photographers in my family on a secret mission to transport people back in time through photographs. Enjoy the ride, but please don't mention it to the IRS.

1957

Harlem, NYC

Even as a pre-teenager, there was nothing ordinary or common about my grandfather – Gavin Grant, Senior. He didn't much like playing with kids his age, preferring to tinker with broken things like watches and car engines. He would tinker until he could repair them like new. Everyone in the neighborhood started to call him Wiz. For a few dollars, he would repair their items and return them in a few days. Granddad saw himself as head of the family after his own father died in World War II. He would give his mother half of his "fix-it" earnings and save the other half for a rainy day.

When Granddad wasn't in school or tinkering with appliances, he admired and found inspiration in three Black men widely celebrated in the community. Two were famous photographers: Victor Van Pelt and Roland Roundtree, and the third was Jazz saxophonist Holland "Shep" Shepherd. Van Pelt taught my grandfather everything there was to know about cameras. He admired Roundtree because he was the first Black man to achieve national success in the photography industry, and lastly, he thought Holland Shepherd was the coolest dude with the slickest style. More importantly however, Holland inadvertently gave him the idea to create the time-travel portal.

My own father, Gavin Grant Jr. idolized his father. Not solely because of the creation of the family's heirloom mystical camera, but also because he used it only for benevolent reasons. Granddad used the camera to help young black men of Harlem in need of a second chance to put their life on the right track. He changed destinies at no cost to the time-traveler, and without publicity or fanfare.

Unlike my granddad, my position is that benevolence doesn't have to be completely free. Decades after Granddad's transition, I finally convinced my father to extend time-travel to more than wayward teenagers on a fast-track to nowhere. Everyone makes mistakes, including those eagerly willing to pay a hefty fee for the opportunity to correct them. So we began offering the service to people who could afford to pay a million dollars to alter their destiny.

Forgive me for getting ahead of the story; let's go back to Gavin Grant Senior, my inventive Granddad. Every day, as a ten year old, he walked the same route to and from school. On one such trip, the sky opened up and he ducked inside a doorway to escape the downpour. It was the ground floor doorway of a storefront photography studio housed in a two-story brownstone apartment building. The studio was closed, but Granddad was mesmerized by the large and glorious black and white photographs centered on easels in the display windows. He lingered until the rain lightened up and then made a mad dash to school.

Walking the same path a few weeks later, he was overjoyed to see a towering, six foot-four inch, elderly Black figure walk into one of the studio's display windows from inside the shop. The man began adjusting portraits, hanging some and removing others. Granddad walked up to the open display window and spoke to the imposing gentleman. "Never saw our people wearing fur coats and riding in a car like that. Are you taking it down?"

"Not now I'm not," Van Pelt said.

Then Van Pelt returns the portrait of Black people wearing their Sunday best - topped off with high hats and mink coats, to the center easel.

"My job is to make sure whippersnappers like you see images of our people living the good life. It happens, not nearly enough for certain, so I need to leave this photo right here," he remarked.

"Who are they Sir?"

"A better question is, who are you young man?" said the elder statesman.

"My name is Gavin."

"Gavin, do you have more than one name?" Gavin looked at him and smiled.

"Yes Sir, I'm Gavin Grant, but everyone calls me Wiz."

"Why is that?"

Gavin simply shrugs his shoulders and directs his eyes toward the ground, as if he's embarrassed to explain how he acquired the nickname.

"Is your preference that I call you Gavin then?" Van Pelt asked.

The young man looked up and nods.

"Good to know you Gavin. I'm Mr. Van Pelt. I need to grab something from inside, follow me If you like."

Gavin has never been inside a photography studio and is beyond excited to check it out. He happily follows the elderly man inside the cramped studio. Heavy furniture fills the room. The walls are covered with portraits of black community leaders and celebrities. A few of the portraits depict the routines of Harlem life.

The photographer turns to the young man and asked, "Do you have a camera?"

Gavin shakes his head no.

The seventy year old man continued, "If you help me out around the shop after school, I'll give you one. Sound good?"

Gavin released a barrage of questions in rapid succession. "Do you own this place? Are you really going to give me a camera, or do I have to pay you for it? What do you need me to do?"

"For starters, keep the windows sparkling clean, the studio dust free, and help me hang portraits wherever there's space," Van Pelt responds. "I can't attract new customers if they can't see my work through the window", he continued.

"Is that all I have to do to get a camera?" Gavin asks.

Mr. Van Pelt shakes his head, No. "I'm going to teach you how to use the camera. If you want to keep it, you need to become a good photographer. Understood?"

"Yes Sir. When can I start?"

"I'll see you when you've discussed it with your parents and they say okay. Now go on and see if the school will let you in at this late hour."

✦ ✦ ✦

"SHE'S NOT A GHOST, SHE'S A DREAM OF WHAT'S TO COME"

It wasn't too long after their first meeting that Granddad showed back up at Van Pelt's photography studio.

"Mom says yes, we could always use the extra money, as long as I do my homework and get chores done. Couldn't ask my father, cause he died in West Virginia when I was a baby. He worked in a coal mine and mom says he had black lungs. We moved here to Harlem right after his funeral. Are you going to give me a camera and pay me to help you?"

Mr. Van Pelt takes a minute to digest all that Gavin shared. "Sorry about your dad. I had family who worked in the Warsaw mines of Kentucky. Good money to be had, but spending all that time underground is dangerous for sure. I'll give you a dollar a week to help out, plus the camera. But remember, it's not a toy. You only get to keep it if you learn how to take good photos."

Gavin is so happy, and then suddenly, his eyes bug out as if he's unsettled by what he sees propped up on a table. He stares at a framed portrait of a couple dressed in wedding attire. There appears to be an apparition of a little girl standing off to the side of the bride and groom.

Gavin forces his fright down long enough to meekly address the photographer. Stammering, he asked: "Uh, Mr. Van Pelt, why is there a ghost in this picture?"

"It's called a portrait Gavin, not a picture. She's not a ghost to that couple young man, simply their beloved daughter."

Gavin's voice is wobbly, and he has an expression of fear on his face. "Looks like a ghost to me."

His uneasiness surprised Mr. Van Pelt and reminds him that his new helper is merely a boy, and is simply too young to grasp the ethereal nature of the photograph.

"The couple wants a child. The girl is a dream of what's to come for them."

"Huh? Why don't they just take a picture, I mean portrait, after she gets here?" Gavin responds in all seriousness.

"Can you read Gavin?"

"I'm ten years old, Sir."

"If that's a yes, there's a verse I wrote to insert into this portrait. It's on the desk in the back room entitled, "*Our Family*". Retrieve it and bring it to me."

Gavin walks a few steps towards the back room and stops. Visibly uncomfortable, he looks at Van Pelt and says, "It's really dark in there."

"Yes, it has to be that way in order to print the photographs. Don't turn on the light or you'll ruin my negatives. The poem should be close to the top of the pile of papers on the desk."

The boy's footsteps are quick. It takes a few minutes for his eyes to get acclimated to the darkness. He scans the room and his gaze rests on the stack of papers on the desktop. He moves swiftly to the pile, finds the poem, dashes out the darkroom, and hands it to his mentor.

Van Pelt takes the portrait of the wedding couple out of its frame, and inserts the brief *Our Family* verse. Holding up the portrait he asks, "Do you see how small this image of the child is compared to her parents?"

"Yes Sir."

"That's done with a projecting machine. I can make different size images, from small to wall-size."

"Really?" Gavin exclaims in amazement.

"It's part of being a good photographer, but I can't teach you how to do it if you're afraid to be in the Darkroom, or are unwilling to learn about free-flowing spirits."

CHAPTER 2

EAST 126TH STREET, HARLEM – 1958

✦

Victor Van Pelt arrives at the prodigious photo session with his protégé Gavin Grant following close behind. Gavin is excited because he's never heard of a professional group-photo essay. Fifty-seven of the greatest jazz musicians in the country pose on the steps of a Brownstone residence. Ten children of varying ages sit curbside in front of the steps. Esquire magazine photographer Art Kane snaps photos of the legendary artists for a spread to appear in a future edition of the publication. Gavin stands alongside Van Pelt and appears to be in a trance as he watches the photo session.

"Why would all these people want to take a photo together?" Gavin asked.

"For one, they're getting paid, and on top of that, they're making history."

Gavin, with total sincerity, remarked, "History, who cares about that?"

Van Pelt chuckles at the youngster's naivety. "You will, in time. Trust me."

In silence, the mentor and young protégé turn their attention back to the photo session. Gavin suddenly darts away from Van Pelt and runs towards the Brownstone. He takes an end seat on the curb alongside the other children. The Esquire photographer doesn't seem to mind Gavin's presence and continues taking snapshots of the group gathered in front of the Brownstone.

The legendary photo session comes to an end. Some of the esteemed musicians chat amongst themselves, others leave the scene.

Van Pelt approaches Gavin. "Little man, I see you like taking chances." Then Van Pelt smiles, pats the back of Gavin's head and makes his way over to the photographer to apologize for Gavin's brashness.

Gavin looks around and he recognizes the noted trumpeter Ace Porter fidgeting with a camera and standing not too far from him. Gavin decides to offer the musician his help and approaches him.

"Mr. Ace, my name is Gavin."

Before Ace can respond, there is a loud commotion. All eyes turn towards the sound. Sharply dressed in a stylish suit and wearing his trademark pork-pie hat, straight shooter, saxophonist Holland Shepherd has arrived, shouting obscenities as he walks through the thinning crowd.

"Where the fuck is everyone going? I thought we were taking a picture," Holland yells at no one in particular.

"Shep, you missed the shot. Why weren't you here on time?" Ace asked, as he calls Holland by the shortened version of his last name.

Without missing a beat, Holland said: "Shit, I never knew there was two ten o'clocks in the motherfucking day."

"Ace lets out a hearty laugh, and notices that a few additional, dressed to impress tardy jazz titans, have just arrived on the block. He turns to Holland and says, "Shep, hold up man".

Then he turns and calls out to the late-comers, "Mose, Charlie, all you cats come over here."

With cool confidence and swag, the musicians walk over to Ace and exchange warm hugs and greetings.

"I need a group picture of you slow risers to document the existence of twin-tens for all you late son of a guns." Childlike and impressionable Gavin is in awe of the men and takes it all in. Out of nowhere a gust of wind swirls underneath Holland Shepherd's hat and forces it to the ground.

"I've never seen a hat like this," Gavin says as he picks it up and attempts to hand it back to Holland.

"If you dig it little man, keep it. I have more than one."

Gavin is speechless. He looks admiringly at Shep, and then down at the pork-pie hat he caresses gently in the palm of his hands. Just as Gavin finds the courage to speak it only comes out slightly above a whisper, "Thank you Mr. Shepherd, I will wear it proudly."

The flamboyant musician has already turned his attention to Porter and doesn't hear Gavin's remarks. "Ace, instead of proving that we were all too late for the official photo, why don't you do something that'll really be worth a damn?"

Ace looks puzzled, "What are you talking about man?"

Holland responds with a straight face and a serious tone, "Make Esquire's camera go backwards to include me in the motherfucking magazine picture with the rest of you cats."

Ace slaps Holland on the back and remarks while laughing, "You're crazy as hell man." Everyone breaks out in laughter except little Gavin, he's lost in thought.

✦ ✦ ✦

CAMERAS ARE WINDOWS TO THE SOUL

Van Pelt and Gavin are busy tidying up the photography studio. In a few hours it will be packed with enthusiastic fans of noted photographer, book author, and all-around Renaissance man Roland Roundtree Jr.

Gavin proudly stated to his mentor, "I finished his book last night."

Van Pelt is surprised and pleased that his young protégé

read the book so quickly, "What did you think about it?"

"It was great. But I don't get why he called it, *CAMERAS DON'T LIE?*"

Van Pelt's head moves as a signal to young Gavin to look towards the front door, as he remarked, "Ask him why he did it yourself, there he is."

Gavin looks up just as the bushy-mustached, distinguished looking Roundtree walks through the door.

"Hey Van, how you been?" Roundtree and Van Pelt embraced, while Gavin stood there with his mouth wide-open and watched in awe.

"Good to see you man. Let me introduce you to young Gavin here. He's my right-hand," Van Pelt said.

Gavin snaps his mouth close. Thanks to his recent growth spurt, he's almost six feet and towers over the legendary photographer, Roundtree. Nevertheless, Gavin humbly extends his hand. "Nice to meet you sir, may I ask you a question?"

The Renaissance man looks at him warmly and replied, "Of course."

"What do you mean cameras don't lie?"

"You cut right to the chase, huh, son? It's simply a metaphor."

Gavin doesn't want to tell Mr. Roundtree that he's clueless about the meaning of the word metaphor, but of course his facial expression betrays him.

Roundtree kindly rescues him, "A metaphor is simply a figure of speech - a different way to say something. In this instance it means that my camera lens always reveals the truth. I can use the camera against what I hate most: racism, intolerance and poverty. Through the lens, I see the real person, their pain and sorrow; as well as their joy and happiness. The true story shows itself in my camera lens."

The young man remains clueless. "When, I look through the camera everything looks the same. There is no story."

Gordon revealed compassion and the wisdom of his years and experience with his response, and said "It takes a lot of looking before you're able to train your eye to see the beauty, or the hidden misery."

"How long did it take you?"

"That's not the right question, Son. Don't ever compare yourself to another. Simply focus on the things that you like or dislike and let the camera show it. That's the photo you want to take. Be different than me or Van Pelt. Feel something about the subject you're photographing and in no time, you'll be telling a story through the lens."

The three men turn their attention to an ordinary looking woman in a waitress uniform as she enters the studio. She wiped her hands on her apron and smiled brightly as her eyes focused on the handsome Roland Roundtree. She swiftly walks over to him and warmly huggs the photographer as if she knows him.

"Mr. Roundtree, I told them at the diner I'd be right back. I had to come over to meet the man who took these pretty pictures of all these fancy clothes." Then she pulled a rolled Life magazine out of her apron pocket.

CHAPTER 3

OAKLAND, CALIFORNIA – 2018

✦

Granddad took over the studio following the death of Mr. Van Pelt and operated it for over thirty years. After my Grandfather passed away, Dad relocated the family photography business from Harlem to Oakland, California and renamed it Custom Memories Photography Studio. We continued to offer family portraits and graduation photos, but the name change was more reflective of our specialty service, TIME TRAVEL.

Granddad's consistent tinkering with the mechanics of things, coupled with his unbridled curiosity with Holland Shepherd's musings to Ace Porter, eventually turned into a mysteriously, tangible creation.

He lived up to his childhood nickname - the "Wiz", and actually invented a camera that can send people through time. The inexplicable nature of the invention is that the special camera transports a person back to the time reflected in any original photograph he had previously taken.

The option to time-travel was only available to wayward teenagers or young adults. Granddad provided them with the opportunity to travel back in time to correct life-altering mistakes by choosing a different action than the one that caused their life to spiral out-of-control. Then they were able to return to the present day to begin life renewed on the right path. Sometimes, the youth was transported simply to escape ramifications of Jim Crow policies, or some other racial injustice about to impact his life at no fault of his own.

Granddad never charged the time traveler a fee for the service. The only stipulation he required of the traveler was to keep the service a secret.

I joined the family business long after granddad's death. After a few years, I convinced Dad to offer time-travel to adults who could afford to pay a hefty price for the service, while still offering it free to juvenile delinquents or utterly directionless youth. Once I painted the picture that the money could help the underserved and economically challenged people within the city, it was an easy sell.

CHAPTER 4

CUSTOM MEMORIES
PHOTOGRAPHY STUDIO

✦

Originally, our business was located on the first floor of our home, similar to the set-up of Mr. Van Pelt's Harlem Studio. Sadly, when a fire erupted in the studio it destroyed both the business and our home. Thereafter, we never lived in the same building that also housed the photography studio.

Custom Memories is now located in a sleek, glass building directly across the street from Oakland's jewel, Lake Merritt. We easily purchased the building a few years after we began charging rich adults for time travel. The lobby is spacious and airy. It features an atrium with large plants, flowers and trees. White furniture and art work contrast the foliage. Along the perimeter, studio rooms are separated by sliding glass walls that can open to create a single room. We use the larger, single room space frequently to host community events or display our photography pieces. We also allow the local chapters of select National non-profit organizations like the Urban League, and Jack and Jill of America to use the lobby for special functions at no charge.

The lobby's receptionist area includes huge portraits of Victor Van Pelt, Roland Roundtree and my Grandfather, Gavin Grant, Senior. Alongside their portraits are smaller prints of their notable works. There's also a sleek, lustrous black marble receptionist counter that we convert to a bar when hosting special events.

The money started rolling into the business once we began to charge a fee for time-travel. Dad and I struggled to come to a mutual agreement on the right price for an opportunity to change life altering mistakes, or to tweak circumstances that placed lives on the wrong path. We finally agreed to set the price high at one million dollars. However, when you think about what's provided for that tidy sum, it's not too high and certainly within reach of many wealthy, good people in search of their true destiny.

Actually it's always been easy to find clients, because everyone makes mistakes and has skeletons in their closets. Some people's misguided blunders or inability to see their own self-worth however, irretrievably alters the trajectory of their lives in a less than desirable manner.

Time-travel clients have always come through our "regular" photography business. We've practically photographed everyone in town through graduation shots, anniversary portraits, and civic or social functions. We snap photos, and form relationships with our repeat clients. Inevitably, through the years people start to reveal regrets and painful experiences. We listen; learn their financial status, discover the character of the person, and gain an appreciation for who can be trusted with our family's secret invention. The information is stored in Dad's and my collective memories.

Most of the money generated from our time-travel service is used to benefit children. Specifically, we help teenagers stand on solid ground when returning from time travel. Additionally, we provide transportation services and Day Care for our elementary aged students.

To the right of the lobby is the Custom Memories Children's Day Care and Photography Club. It's important that the children see likeness of themselves when they walk into the facility; therefore, large portraits of famous African Americans hang prominently. On another wall, hangs a variety of child-themed photographs in bold colored frames. We call it: "Our Wall of Fame."

Once a week I teach photography to the little tykes, ages four and five. Today is that day, and I enter the room to see twenty-five beautiful smiling faces sitting quietly. Nikon Coolpix cameras rest on the tables in front of each child.

"Good morning everyone," I said cheerfully.

"Good morning Ms. Grant," the little bright-eyed, sweet voiced darlings respond in harmony.

"I'm happy to see you all this morning. Let's begin as we always do, reciting our photography rules. What's rule number one?"

The children respond loudly in unison, "My eyes are the best photography equipment."

"Number two?"

"I don't take a photograph, I make a photograph."

"Three?"

"Everything and everyone is photogenic."

"Excellent, what's the next rule?"

"Even bad photos are good photos."

"That's right, because?"

"Every photo tells a story."

Every student remembers the rules and can recite them upon request. I'm so proud of them and take a moment to look at these enthusiastic little sponges. They are going to be expert photographers running around snapping magnificent photos. A few of them hopefully, may even work for Custom Memories some day.

"Well done children, just great. Now who wants to present their story?"

The children enthusiastically began waving photographs of toys, people and animals in the air. Sophia, a low-spirited little girl, stood up. She started to talk but cast her eyes downward towards the floor, as if she's speaking to it.

She said, "Ms. Gisele, I didn't get to share my story before."

"Well then Sophia, now is your turn."

Sophia slowly picks her head up and shows everyone a photograph. She said, "This is my dog Brutus."

"What's the story there, Sweetheart?" I asked.

"Can't you tell that his eyes are sad?" she said.

A little boy named Troy chimes in and said exactly what I was thinking. "He doesn't look sad to me. Why do you think your dog looks sad?"

Sophia said, "Cause he knew he wouldn't see me anymore."

Troy responded before I could inquire, "Why not?"

"He was hit by a car and now he's dead," Sophia manages to mumble as the sounds of her sobs grew louder than her proclamation.

The children all gasped. Sophia cried harder and I quickly moved to her side and hugged her tight. Troy hasn't finished with his interrogation. "Is death forever Ms. Gisele?"

I said, "Love is forever, and death can't take that away. Brutus will always be in Sophia's heart." I hand Sophia a tissue, and then scan all the sad faces on the children. "The best photographs tell a story that moves something in you. They can make you happy or sad. Don't you all agree that Sophia's photo tells a compelling story?"

The children nod in unison, like sad little robots. Troy raises his hand, he's contrite now. "Ms. Gisele, don't you think Brutus' photo should be on our Wall of Fame?"

"Yes. Why don't you help Sophia find a spot for him."

Troy grabs Sophia's hand and together they walk over to the wall. They stick a push-pin through it, hang the dog's photo, and slowly return to their seats. However, the always inquisitive Troy is not yet finished with his questions. He said, "Sophia gets the prize too, right?"

"Of course, that's the rule if your photo is on the Wall of Fame. Sophia, hand me your camera." I reach down inside the cabinet and retrieve two small gold charms, replicas of the ones hanging on a delicate chain around my neck. One charm is a camera and the other is a rose. I place the charms on a metal ring hanging from the camera's lanyard and slide it over Sophia's head.

"Class is over for today. Put your photographs away inside your desk and we'll cover more next week. "

Customary at the conclusion of class, I hug each child. As I attempt to exit the room, Troy catches me off guard. He said, "Smile Ms. Gisele." I turn to see Troy pointing his camera at me. I'm irritated and instinctively put my hand up to block my face.

"Troy, don't. Stop. No photos of me." I said with more force than I should have.

The little boy is startled by the bluntness of my refusal. The rest of the children look on confused and I leave the room in a huff, embarrassed by my inability to follow my own rules. Specifically, rule number three states, everything and everyone is photogenic. But I never thought the kids would try and take my photo, and I certainly couldn't allow it, not with this ugly facial burn spread across my face. All these years later since the house caught on fire, and I still have not grown comfortable with my appearance and this damn scar.

As soon as I step in the hallway, Ms. Robbie – the students' opinionated and feisty regular pre-school teacher, greets me. "You're stopping a little early today, are my babies okay?"

"They're fine, but had to swallow a hard lesson. They learned nothing stays the same but a snapshot," I said wryly while I used my hand to ensure my side bangs are covering the burn. I started the walk towards my office and Ms. Robbie called after me.

"Sounds like a dreary lesson for four and five year olds. Hope next week's lesson is more uplifting," she bellowed.

I flashed a thumb up without turning around to face her, and sauntered through the glass doors labeled GISELE GRANT, PHOTOGRAPHER.

My office is a stark mix of old and new. There is an actual green metal - 126th New York City street sign sticking out of an exposed brick wall. It's a replica from Granddads' original address. Each corner of the office holds an antique camera braced on tripods. Custom shelving lines the walls and hold framed portraits that Custom Memories has snapped through the years. The furniture is white and matches the seating in the lobby area.

Chuddy Dunn - Oakland's Chamber of Commerce President and my life-long, street wise, smart and charismatic best friend – sits patiently and rolls an unlit cigar between his top lip and nose. A couple of Styrofoam cups rest on the office table in front of him. I'm happy to see him, but you wouldn't know it by what comes out of my mouth. I said, "You're not smoking are you?"

He hands me one of the cups, and calmly remarks. "So you can chew my head off?"

"Is this a Chai-Tea latte?"

"Have you started drinking something else? Hello to you too Ms. Grant, and you're welcome."

"Sorry Chuddy, thanks for thinking of me." I studied his face for a few moments. He had a weird, kind of puzzled expression. "What's the matter? You look strange."

"Strange? It's the same look I have every time I enter this building."

I chuckled, "You're still trying to come to terms with traveling back in time, after all these years?"

He smiled. His face is a map of bewilderment. "All I have to do is get close to this building and damn near lose my cool Black man status."

"Didn't know I moved you like that," I respond but only partly in jest. I'm actually flirting, even though he never notices my attempts. This time is no different. He simply sips from his coffee cup. "Anyway, it was decades ago Chuddy."

"Listen sis, I didn't believe it could be done then, and I'm still amazed - but grateful, that it was."

I smile at him. "Time-travelers always doubt it at first, but you're the only one who has remained freaked out."

"Yeah well, I've always been different. Back in the day, I did everything fast, including self-destruction. Now though - you know, I'm all about slow and steady."

"You – slow? I don't know about that." I suck my teeth at his revelation.

"You know your Dad saved my life. I'd be a fool not to slow down."

I have to catch myself from looking longingly at him, so I take a long sip of my Chai-tea. "You've never been a fool. Besides, you saved yourself. His photograph just provided the opportunity."

"Sure I saved myself, along with that little thing known as your Grandfather's loosely defined magic invention."

"Who needs a definition? It is what it does."

Chuddy smiled, leaned over and kissed my cheek. Then, he gently kissed my other cheek with the scar and walked out of my office. I stood in the doorway, watched him as he stopped in the lobby to speak to the receptionist, Hanna, and then he exited the building.

Later that evening on my way home, I decide to take a detour and check on little Sophia. She and her mother live across town in an apartment on Spencer Street a few blocks from the Oracle Arena. I actually met Sophia and her mother Brenda, at the Arena. Custom Memories purchased a block of tickets for the Disney On Ice holiday show and donated them to the community. The mother and daughter duo were two of the ticket recipients.

Brenda answered the door and greeted me warmly. Their small apartment was sunny and inviting. Photographs of Sophia, her mother and their dog Brutus were everywhere.

"Hi Brenda, hope I'm not interrupting dinner or something. I wanted to see how Sophia was doing?"

Sophia rushes into the room when she hears my voice call out her name.

"Ms. Gisele?" Sophia screeches in a high pitched voice,

surprised to see me standing in her living room. She hugs me.

"She's fine Ms. Grant. She told me she was able to tell the class that we lost Brutus."

As soon as Brenda mentions the dog, Sophia's eyes begin to tear up. Her mother tries to comfort her. I whisper in her mother's ear an offer to take them shopping for a new puppy. Brenda nods enthusiastically. A wide smile fills her face.

"How about I pick you and Sophia up on Saturday morning? We can visit the Oakland Animal shelter to see who may need a home." The three of us embrace.

CHAPTER 5

A DAY IN THE LIFE ROOM

✦

I walked over to the receptionist counter to greet Hanna, who's sorting the mail. Hanna is twenty-one years old and a stunner. She's very sweet, petite and flawlessly fashionable with a style reminiscent of Harlem Renaissance glamour of yesteryear. She projects an image that's in sync with our glass building, beautiful atrium and works of art. "Good Morning Hanna."

Hanna looks up, hands me the mail and replies, "Morning boss."

I scan through the envelopes and then toss them onto her desk behind the marble countertop. "Recycle those. Come with me for a few minutes."

Hanna hops to my side and together we stride thru the atrium area and enter the studio door labeled: A DAY IN THE LIFE. Two of my staff handymen are in close proximity to a floor-to-ceiling sized facial portrait of a dark-haired woman with penetrating eyes. The guys jump as I open the door. "Hey fellas, why are you so jittery?"

The younger of the two men lets out a chuckle. He is Cameron Campbell and is twenty-five years old. He's an awkward, self-deprecating nice guy who is typically reluctant to show anything remotely resembling weakness in front of the older man, his supervisor. His supervisor is Zephaniah Williams, everyone calls him Zeph. He's in his forties, has a slender dancer's physique and when not working for Custom Memories shows his snake oil salesman persona. His reputation in the streets, according to Chuddy, is that of a womanizing hustler.

Cameron pats the mural and responds, "Hi Ms. Grant, one of us is just a little spooked by Ms. Creepy eyes here."

Zeph climbs a ladder, takes a cutting knife from the tool belt around his waist, and reaches towards the mural's face. "I was just about to rip out her pupils so the kid here doesn't wet his pants." Cameron is clearly embarrassed by Zeph's comments, but I didn't really have time to come to his defense.

"Wait, don't cut it Zeph," I yelled at him a little louder than necessary. I just wanted to make sure he didn't ruin the mural.

Zeph turned to me with a confused expression, but he did pause the cutting knife in mid-air.

"Ms. Grant, it's the best way for me to take it down."

"Not if you have to put it back up," I said.

"That's a first. We've never taken a mural down and re-plastered it on the wall," Zeph remarks as he repositions his knife back into his tool bet. He climbs off the ladder and walks over to the closet.

I shrug my shoulders, "Wonders never cease around here huh, Zeph?"

Zeph said," Sure you're right," and retrieves a piece of equipment from the closet. Hanna moves out of the shadows and speaks up.

"What's that?"

"Hey pretty lady," Zeph remarked as he seemed to undress Hanna with his eyes. "It's called a steamer."

I decided to pretend that I didn't notice Zeph's crude expression. I smile at Hanna, place my arm around her shoulder to denote I will protect her, and direct my remarks to both guys. "Let me introduce Hanna, our new Receptionist."

Zeph smirks and continues to leer at Hanna, while Cameron smiles as if he's instantly smitten. Both behaviors render Hanna uncomfortable and she folds her arms across her body with uneasiness.

"We came in today through the back door and apparently missed this pretty young lady altogether. How ya doing?" said Zeph. Hanna manages a slight smile but doesn't respond.

"Hanna that's Zeph, and Cameron's his assistant. They both make sure this place looks good; windows sparkle, paint's fresh, the plants are watered, and of course other duties as assigned." Everyone started laughing.

Cameron stops laughing first and simply gazes at Hannah for a moment. Then he said, "Your beautiful, sparkling eyes would look great on a mural."

Hanna points to barely perceptible acne on her forehead. "No way could I handle seeing these zits wallpaper sized."

"Trust me when I tell you, no one will notice," Cameron said warmly.

"She doesn't have to worry about acne showing or not showing on a mural here, because she'll never be a Day In The Life client of Custom Memories."

I wasn't attacking her, just speaking truth to the universe in how I wanted it to be. I glance over at Hanna and she's looking down at the floor. The guys don't know how to respond either. Then, in an attempt to come to Hanna's defense, Cameron breaks the icy silence in the room. "It would be torture for me anyway, to eventually have to rip Hanna's pretty face off this wall, like we're about to do now for Ms. Creepy eyes here."

"Really," I said to Cameron. I'm already tired of his flirtatious remarks to our new staff member, and sick of the lecherous way Zeph continues to glare at her. I shoot both guys an expression of displeasure. "Zeph, when you're finished taking down the mural, roll it up and put it into an empty cylinder."

"Should I place it in storage?"

"No, just give it to Hanna, and she'll let you know when to put it back up," I said with such a sever tone that Zeph finally received the message.

Zeph turns and taps Cameron on his shoulder and winks on the sly. "Watch how you speak around the ladies. There's a time and place for flirting, and work ain't it." Then Zeph begins to spray the mural with the steamer.

Cameron looks at Hanna and me and offers an apology, "I'm really sorry if I offended either of you." He steps up on the ladder and begins gingerly peeling the mural off the wall.

Once we exit the room, I can see Hanna is nervous. She's uncomfortable but manages to talk to me. "Can Custom Memories' employees also be clients?"

"Sure."

"Then why don't you want to photograph me?"

"I'll take your portrait that's not a problem. I just won't need to turn your portrait into a mural. Most times people regret that they are a DAY IN THE LIFE client.

"I don't understand."

"That's okay, you don't need to." Without further clarification, I proceed down the hallway. Hanna calls after me.

"Ms. Grant, your first appointment is waiting for you in the Moments Room." I shoot her thumbs up without turning around.

Cameron quietly comes out of the DAY IN THE LIFE room. He approaches Hanna from behind and whispers in her ear. "I want to apologize again. I'm not usually crude."

Hanna turns to face him, "No worries. I wasn't actually offended, more like surprised by all the attention."

"Honestly though, it messes me up."

"What does?"

"I don't know any other way to say it Hanna, but it's your beauty. You are fine." Cameron looks nervous and begins to stammer, "Being in your presence is uh…something. "

Hanna is flattered. She blushes and looks at him with brighter, smiling eyes.

CHAPTER 6

CAN HE LIFT HIS FIST OFF HER FACE?

✦

We're in the Moments Room, and I'm preparing to photograph a young couple, Vaughn Price and Kay Hunt, as soon as my assistant completes applying their make-up. They are soon to be married, and requested a portrait to be featured in the wedding invitation.

I embrace the couple in a bear hug. "Good to see you lovebirds. Let's get started on blowing your wedding guests away."

Vaughn replied, "Won't take much effort Gisele, we only need to impress about fifteen people. That's all we can afford to invite."

Kay is mortified. She elbows Vaughn in his ribs. "Don't listen to him Gisele. We're going to need two hundred printed."

"What are you talking about Babe? That's not in our budget."

"Daddy's paying for the photos and invitations. He'll cover all the wedding expenses if you let him."

He scrunched up his facial expression into this weird kind of pained grimace and said, "I'm not sure he can he lift his fist off your Mother's face long enough to pay the invoices associated with our wedding?"

Clearly embarrassed, Kay's steely eyes shoot daggers towards Vaughn. "Really, you had to go there?" Vaughn's facial expression doesn't change. He continues to look like he smells something rotten.

I realized I needed to act quickly before the session gets to the point of no return. "Come on now you two, where's the love? We're here to capture those moments." I pose the couple on a love seat in front of a white muslin Backdrop and click the camera lens. After several clicks in rapid succession, I stop. My energetic assistant, Avery, doesn't miss a beat.

"Where would you like me to position them next Ms. G?"

I point to a place on the marble floor. Avery re-positions the couple to the spot and moves an Umbrella Light Reflector closer to their faces. I nod towards long-stem roses resting in corner vase. Just as quickly, Avery catches my signal and begins to scatter the flowers on the floor surrounding Vaughn and Kay. He speaks to the couple as he artfully places the roses. "Great portraits don't just happen, the boss thinks of everything."

Vaughn laughs. "This isn't our first time at the rodeo. We've used Custom Memories to document all our major milestones."

Avery laughs. "Every client says the same thing, it's like we've photographed the entire city."

I step up on a foot stool and begin shooting Vaughn and Kay from various angles. After a dozen or so clicks I step down to look inside the camera at the shots taken. "Camera is picking up tension on your faces. I don't like these shots. Let's go outside across the street to the Lake and get some sun."

Lake Merritt is beautiful, especially during this time of day. The change in the couple is instantly apparent. They are relaxed and playful. I shoot photos of them feeding the ducks swimming in the Lake; frolicking around the large Greek columns; embracing each other while sitting on a stone bench; and lastly, enjoying a Gondola ride on the lake.

Back inside the studio's Moments room, the young lovers hug me. I tell them softly that, "Portraits should reflect the story you want revealed. We finally uncovered your story outside today."

Kay breaks free of the group hug and reaches behind the muslin backdrop. She pulls out her tote bag and reaches inside. "I almost forgot, Mom asked me to give you something."

"I know it's time for me to shoot your parents' Silver Anniversary portrait."

"Mom wanted me to give you this and said to postpone their Anniversary portrait for awhile, because she wants to schedule a solo session." Kay finds what she was searching for in her tote bag, "Here it is." She hands it to Gisele. It's a small, old and frayed photograph of the Mona Lisa-eyes mural that was on the wall in the DAY IN THE LIFE studio room. It is Kay's Mother, Ramona Hunt.

I look down at the photograph of her mother's youthful face and smile. "My father shot this photo at least two decades ago."

Vaughn chimes in, "Honey your mom looks sad even then. Wonder if that was taken before she was married to your father?"

"Yeah, they were already married. But can you knock it off? I'm pretty tired of your negative remarks about my Dad." She turned to me and managed a weak little smile. "Mother said she'll let you know when they're ready for the Anniversary portrait, but to schedule her solo session during the week following our wedding."

CHAPTER 7

WEDDING RECEPTION KNOCK-OUT

✦

Everything speaks elegance in the Claremont Hotel ballroom. White linen covers the tables and chairs. Silver-framed keepsake portrait center-pieces, of Vaughn and Kay frolicking on Lake Merritt, are strategically placed on the tables in front of each name card. Several tables lining the walls are stacked high with beautifully wrapped wedding presents. The well-dressed guests stop in their tracks to turn and witness Vaughn and Kay's first dance as a married couple.

Then we hear the disc jockey speak loudly into the microphone, "Parents of the Bride and Groom, please join the newlyweds on the dance floor."

A smooth and soulful rendition of John Coltrane's Sentimental Mood is playing through the speakers. The groom's parents, the Prices, are the first to join the couple. The bride's parents, Ramona and Edwin Hunt, walk slowly towards the dance floor. He's fifty, and a big bearish looking brute of a man. She's forty-six, petite in size, and typically timid and docile. We've already seen her big, deep-set, sad eyes on the mural.

As they dance, Edwin speaks to his wife in his usual, repugnant tone and manner. "You look like shit."

"You're still the charmer."

"Why couldn't you wear the dress I picked out?"

"Cause I wore this one, fuck you."

"Can't you at least show some class. This is our daughter's wedding and everyone is looking."

"What the hell do you think this is, if not classy restraint? Do you actually think I want to be here in the middle of the floor with my arms wrapped around your stupid ass?"

"Lower your voice, or I'll --

She cuts him off in the middle of his remarks. "You'll what, knock me out? Been there, done that."

The music ends. Enthusiastic applause erupts. Some guests happily resume eating and others mill around. The groom's parents approach the Hunts. Mom Price said, "Sentimental Mood is our favorite song." The Hunts don't say a word.

Then Mr. Price playfully yet forcefully slaps Edwin on his back. "Coltrane perfectly captures everyone's feelings today, huh Bro?"

The groom's parents are too elated to notice the Hunts' sullenness and lack of response. They reach out and grab the Hunts in a long, warm embrace. Ramona looks up and spots Gisele standing alone snapping shots of the festivities from an opposite corner of the room. She breaks free of the embrace and joins Gisele.

"You know, I simply wanted to see my baby full of joy on her wedding day."

It's good to see Ramona at her daughter's wedding, yet she doesn't look half as happy as I expected. "I'd say your mission is accomplished then".

"Please put my mural back up."

"When?"

"They're off on the honeymoon for two weeks, let's do it before they return."

I nod and gently push Ramona towards the festivities. "Understood, now go soak up some of your daughter's bliss and let me capture those moments in a few snapshots." Ramona turns away from me and walks towards the guests. I call out to her. "Ramona", she pivots around and I complete my thought, "You're wearing that dress. You look beautiful."

Ramona pauses in silence for a few minutes. Finally, sunshine spreads all over her face. "Thank you, two out of three ain't bad."

I had no idea what she was referencing, but remained silent and just smiled at her. She looked joyful and rejoined the other revelers.

CHAPTER 8

RAMONA IS NOT MONA LISA

✦

We're in the studio's DAY IN THE LIFE room. Ramona smiles at her face on the mural. I patiently watch her gather her thoughts. Our time-travel clients always feel an uncontrollable desire to explain themselves right before embarking on the journey.

"I wired the million dollars to the Custom Memories account."

I nod, "Yes, the bank sends deposit alerts to my phone."

"I apologize for the delay, needed more time to sneak money transfers between accounts."

"Are you ready Ramona?" She ignores the question and keeps talking. "He didn't show me his ugly side until after we married. Bad days at work would coax it out of him and direct it my way. After awhile, it didn't need persuasion. Soon as he came home he would start in on me as if I was the cause of his problems. He would smack me around before he started drinking, and be more brutal after. I was young, scared, and didn't know how to stand up to him."

"You did the best you could."

Ramona slides her hand across the mural. She's slipping into depressive thoughts. "Look at my sad and creepy eyes pleading for help because my mouth couldn't."

I realize I have to ease her out of self-pity and around to the business of returning to the past, back to the original moment she declined to alter her destiny.

"Are you sure you're ready to do this now, do you need more time?"

"My dignity has waited too long as it is."

I gesture for her to sit down alongside me on the opposite side of the room. "We need to revisit the rules."

Ramona sits, and sounding like a drill sergeant, I begin reciting time travel requirements. "You cannot remain in the past. You must return to the exact landing spot within twenty-four hours. Lastly, this photo is your portal back here to the present day. Clutch it against your chest when you're ready to return." She gives me a strange look. I hand her the small photographed likeness of the enlarged mural.

"Twenty-four hours is not a great deal of time," she said.

Her remarks explain her weird facial expression. "It's all you'll need to change the action, or in your case, the lack of action, that put you where your life is now."

"If I fail, can I try it another time?"

I shake my head. "This is it Ramona. You get one do-over."

"What will happen if I take longer than the twenty-four hours?"

"Nothing good."

She stares at me, "For instance?"

"The photograph disintegrates, and then your body will join it."

She doesn't flinch, and frankly surprises me with her response.

"Shit, is that all? I'm used to being pulverized, twenty plus years to be exact. It's been my constant companion. So if I don't make it back, I'll just be normalized."

"Not really, but anyway there will be consequences for us here at Custom Memories as well."

Ramona's voice is no longer strong and cocky, it wobbles. She expresses concern. "What kind of consequences? I wouldn't want anything to happen to you or your father."

"Then comply with the rules. Do you agree to return within twenty-four hours?"

"Yes," she said with conviction.

"If you're ready, then stand with your back flush to the mural and clutch the photo to your chest."

Ramona follows my command.

"Remember Ramona, when you get there everything, including your husband, will be as it was."

She looks me straight in the eye and says confidently, "I won't be the same. Let's do this."

I aim the family heirloom – Granddad's supernatural camera, at Ramona and click. She disappears.

CHAPTER 9

YEAR 1992 - CALM DOWN AND GIVE ME THE KNIFE

◆

The small apartment was filled with modest furniture. It was immaculate, nothing appeared out of place. A twenty-one year old Ramona Hunt, holding an infant on her lap, talks on the phone. "Wish he were more like you Dad, but he's always angry. It's scary at times."

"I'll talk to him. Call me again after he's come home and you've eaten dinner."

"No that's okay Dad. If I can't get through to him tonight, the baby and I will just come home to you and mom." The baby begins to cry.

"It sounds like she doesn't like that idea," her Dad chuckles.

"She's cranky. I couldn't get her to take her afternoon nap. I'll talk to you later daddy." Ramona walks towards the kitchen and places the crying baby in a playpen. She puts a pacifier in little Kay's mouth, but the baby simply spits it out and continues to cry. Ramona turns her attention to the stove and stirs pots. She's startled by the sound of a door opening and slamming shut. She gathers herself together and said, "Hi honey, we're in the kitchen."

Edwin walks through the apartment and pauses in front of the dining table. He scowls at the food-less plate settings. Edwin enters the kitchen and picks up the wailing baby from the play-pen. He kisses little Kay, and coos over her, then he turns and barks at Ramona, "Don't you see she's crying?"

"I can hear her too. She's just tired, couldn't get her to take a nap."

Edwin returns the baby to the play-pen and approaches Ramona. She puckers her lips for a kiss. He smacks her solidly across her cheek. "Your job is to keep her from crying."

As a reflex, both of Ramona's hands move to cradle her cheek. In pain, she stares up at her husband's menacing expression. He hauls off and hits her hard on the other cheek and said, "Have my dinner ready and on the table when I get home."

A hysterical Ramona slides down to the floor. Collecting herself, she clinches her teeth, grabs hold of the counter top and pulls herself up into a standing position.

"Hurry up and bring my dinner. I'm hungry."

Ramona begins plating his food from the pots. She notices the long-blade knife in the butcher block and slides it out. Holding it tightly she points it directly at Edwin.

"What are you going to do with that?" Edwin asks her in a sort of sarcastic, bemused tone.

Ramona does not cower or back down. She extends her arm towards her husband's gut and grips the knife handle like a dagger. "Put your hands on me again and you'll find out."

Edwin is angry, yet simultaneously surprised and intrigued by Ramona's newfound obstinacy. He's hesitant to call her bluff. "No need to flip out."

"Interesting how consistent slaps across one's face will do that to you."

He is beyond out of patience with her, "Well if you would just do shit right, I wouldn't have to teach you a lesson."

Rage poured out of her, "Let me be the first to tell you that you're a lousy fucking teacher."

"Calm down and give me the knife Ramona."

Ramona stands strong and steadfast in her resolve. She doesn't move a muscle and continues to point the knife at her husband. "Listen to me when I tell you, I am not a rest stop for your restless fists. If you ever hit me again, you better not go to sleep."

"Are you finished now? Have you gotten everything off your chest?

"No. You do know that this is a community property state, right?"

Edwin looks at her in disbelief. He's never been on the receiving end of such venom, like he's accustomed to dishing it out. He doesn't know what to do, so he simply storms out of the room and out of the apartment.

Ramona looks at the wall clock, reaches inside her purse and pulls out the small photograph used for her Custom Memories' mural. She clutches the photo tightly against her chest.

CHAPTER 10

YEAR 2018 - SHE'S A SURVIVOR

✦

Gisele's dad - Gavin Grant, Jr. eats lunch in the midst of a crowded restaurant's controlled chaos. Gavin is dressed like men of a by-gone era. He wears a sharp, three piece suit and a matching fedora. He's joined by his friend and accountant, John Watson, who is in an outfit that was never stylish.

"I'll go with you to the Internal Revenue Bureau," John advised his friend.

"Thanks man, but Gisele wants to handle it herself."

"It should be a quick, slam-dunk meeting. They simply want clarification on your client fee schedules."

Gavin looks his friend up and down and said, "I wish you would clarify why you're wearing that jacket?"

"What? This is cashmere man, I got it for a steal."

Gavin reaches over, fingers John's lapel, and mumbles sarcastically, "No doubt."

"You wouldn't know a bargain unless it was buried in the Old Testament."

The two friends chuckle, "And you wouldn't know what's in the Old Testament."

So what's going on with Gisele these days? Is she dating yet?

Gavin shrugs and his playful banter quickly turned to one of concern. "She works too much. She's still ballroom dancing with the dude that's no good, and won't admit her feelings for the one that is."

"Relax Gavin, when she wants more, she'll go after it."

"From your mouth to God's ears, you know she shares the same discontentment with life that her mother had."

John listens to him in earnest. Gavin looks off into space with sorrowful eyes. He's reliving his painful memories for the millionth time. "The fire just consumed the place within minutes after Gisele and her mother were rescued."

"Did Cozette pass away in the hospital?"

Gavin shakes his head, "She died in the ambulance and lived an unfulfilled life."

"Why would you say that? Wasn't she living her dream working the New York and San Francisco fashion shows?"

"In her mind, the best worked in the city of lights and romance."

"Paris?"

Gavin looks broken. He simply nods his head.

"She was beautiful of course, but never more so than when she was talking about you and Gisele. Paris runways could never light her up like that."

"We take portraits of special moments for other people. She wanted to create her own in France."

John said, "Life is a trade-off."

Gavin erupts at the pain of remembering, "My wife's life was snatched in a flash and at the same time our baby girl's confidence was exchanged for facial scars." He rubs the side of his face. "Gisele's ashamed of her looks. Instead of seeing her scars as a survivor's badge, she's insecure. Some trade-off, huh?"

John searches for something to say and knew whatever he uttered would be inadequate. He simply said, "Give her time."

"I'm getting old. I want her to have love before the Almighty calls me home."

"Getting old? You still can't count my friend, no wonder the IRS wants to check your numbers."

John's humor is just what Gavin needs, both men laugh heartily. A waitress walks up and attempts to hand Gavin the bill, he stops her and points to John. "You need to give that to Mr. Math wiz over there." The men and the waitress laugh. She complies with the direction, clears the table and exits.

John quickly turns serious. He folds his hands behind his head, sits up and looks directly into Gavin's eyes and said, "Didn't you just say Gisele is a survivor? When are you going to believe it?"

Gavin appreciates his friend's advice and agrees with him. He says he'll try to relax about Gisele's romantic life.

"I'm more worried about your lack of companionship, than your daughter's. You know my wife has been trying to fix you up with her sister," John said.

"What does she look like these days? It's been years since I last saw Lisa."

John pulls out his cell phone and scans through the photos searching for Lisa's picture. He locates a photo of his wife Laura standing next to Lisa and shows his friend.

"Hmmm, she looks better than I remember. Ask Laura what day and time is dinner? "

CHAPTER 11

WHITE DUST

✦

It's Friday evening. I pull into a parking space in front of a large warehouse building. It is directly across the road from a concrete manufacturing plant. Tiny little white dust particles cover everything. When I walk into the spacious, mirrored ballroom, the usual couples are already here and warming up. An instructor is in the front of the room searching for music on an IPad docking station.

The sounds of big band music come through the speakers. Couples begin to Lindy Hop. Zeph barely gives me time to put my purse down and change into my dancing shoes before he grabs my arm. I'm not complaining though, he is strong, nicely built and flexible. He leads me with beautiful fluid movements, which makes it that much worse when I step on his feet. "Sorry, I can't seem to focus. My mind is at work."

"Look around Gisele, if you haven't noticed, we're not in your studio. Stop trying to lead. Here, in my building, I'm the boss." His voice is a little too cocky, but I overlook it because he's the only one I know who loves ballroom and step-dancing as much as I do.

The music transitions to a faster paced song – Black Magic Woman. I'm in heaven and we salsa to the beats like paid professionals.

Dance class is over and I accompany Zeph to his office. The space is in disarray, with papers and stuff everywhere. He dials a code to open a vault hidden behind a bookcase. The vault is stuffed and bursting at the seams. He takes out one of the tiny, clear plastic bags full of white powder. He pours the contents on the desk and snorts some of it up his nose. I just stand there watching.

Zeph said, "You want some?"

I shake my head. "Never acquired a taste, but aren't you afraid to leave that stuff here in your office?"

"It's in the vault, besides this is where it should be for easy access for my customers."

"What customers? You mean the dance students?"

"No. No. My best customers work right across the street."

"At the cement plant?"

Zeph snorts the remaining cocaine, then he looks at me like I'm an alien. He wipes his face with the back of his hand and nods. "Their noses clog-up breathing the wrong powder all day, so they stop here at the end of their shift for a toot of the right stuff."

"They should wear face mask while working to protect their noses."

He gives me that alien look again. "What? Lady, you are too deep for me."

I follow him into another part of the warehouse, which he's converted into a residential loft. It's quite nice actually. We're sitting on the couch, drinking wine. I surprise myself and begin talking about my mother. "She was so beautiful."

"So are you."

I'm uncomfortable with his compliment and look away. Zeph refills my glass. I continue my story, "She was a model and used to dress me in matching outfits."

"Guess you liked that huh, twin clothes?"

I shrug my shoulders and gulp down my drink. "She did, I wanted to make her happy". I pour myself another glass of the last of the wine.

Zeph goes to the cabinet to grab another bottle. He fills his glass and pats my shoulder, "Well at least you shared sweet family memories to keep you smiling. It's more than most of us have."

I can feel my eyes welling up with tears, "What do the crappy ass memories do for us?"

Zeph chugs down his glass and moves in closer to me. "I'm not following, what do you mean?"

"My mother never once complimented me and to her hugging was a federal crime."

"Hugs aren't all that they're cracked up to be."

"They are to a little kid. Would you believe she would just step aside if I came towards her like I wanted to hug?"

Then, Zeph leaned over and whispered in my ear, "Hmm, an iceberg underneath her beauty. Ice met fire, interesting end of life Karma."

Instantly, his remark angered me, and whatever buzz I was feeling from the wine disappeared. "Karma? My mother didn't deserve death because she didn't want to hug me."

"Did I say she did?

I felt a need to strike out to hurt him as his insensitive, thoughtless remark pained me, "Do you even know the definition of the word Karma?"

"Don't insult me Gisele, you know you're twisting my words and intent."

It must be reliving the memories that moved me to brush the hair away from my face, which I never do in front of anyone, and begin to caress the scars. "I was seven when the fire broke out. What did I do to deserve this disfigurement?"

Zeph attempts to trace my scars with his lips. I hastily move away from him and in a biting tone I said "What are you doing? Don't do that."

Surprised by my harshness, he responds in kind. "Everybody has scars, some emotional, some physical and some people have both. Instead of making me miserable, why don't you talk to a shrink and find a fucking plastic surgeon."

As calmly as I can muster I respond, "That's surprising?"

Zeph grabs the wine bottle and gulps down its remains. "What's that?"

I jump off the couch and walk towards the door. "Finally, there's something out of your mouth that has a semblance of sense."

He looks high and crazed, "Ugly psycho bitch, didn't really want you anyway. Get the fuck out."

I gladly comply and slam the door behind me.

Zeph returns to his office and opens the vault. He scoops up bags of cocaine and tosses them into a container on top of the bookcase. It's almost time for a shift change at the cement factory, and he never reveals the location of his vault or stash of drugs in front of his clients. Then he retrieves a handgun from the vault and slips it into the front of his pants, leaving the handle visible from his waistband.

The doorbell rings right on time. It's his first customer of the night.

The rest of the weekend I prepare my IRS presentation materials. I arrived at work early Monday morning and stopped at Hanna's receptionist station. Glad to see she's already here. As unpleasant as the Friday exchange between Zeph and me was, I knew he would come in to work anyway. I imagine his coked-out mind will think it was no big deal. "Hanna, I have a few appointments today and won't be back until tomorrow. I need you to give this to Zeph when he arrives."

Hanna takes the envelope from my outstretched hand. "Good Morning Boss, anything I should tell him?"

"No it's all explained in the letter inside. But, for your information, today is his last day. Security will be here to escort him out at the end of the workday."

CHAPTER 12

SPEAKING DIFFERENT LANGUAGES

✦

Internal Revenue Bureau Agent Leland Brewer is timid and sort of clumsy. He juggles an arm full of files and enters the Director's office. He takes a seat at a desk opposite his gruff boss, the Bureau Director Charles Knox. The always unpleasant Knox speaks first. "The tip we received was sketchy on the details but money laundering allegations usually prove true." Leland adjusts his out-of-style eyeglasses and responds, "They haven't missed any filings."

Knox forces an obviously fake smile, "What does that have to do with unreported income?"

Leland drops a few files and clumsily retrieves them. "I spoke with Custom Memories' bankers and accountant."

"Maybe they're all in it together. Have you looked into their filings?"

Leland stares at his boss in disbelief. "You're kidding right?"

"Think about it. She's a photographer in Oakland California, not New York, not Los Angeles. Yet she generates millions in revenue. Why?"

Leland stammers, "They have a lot of wealthy clients?"

Knox frowns. "Pretty naïve aren't you? You could never do my job."

The phone on Knox's desk rings. He answers. "Send her in."

Leland rises and extends his hand to greet me as I enter the office. "Good morning Ms. Grant. I'm Leland Brewer and this is Director Charles Knox. Please have a seat." Leland points to a chair at the conference table. He and Knox join me as I sit at the conference table. Leland continues talking to put me at ease, "It seems your studio has photographed almost everyone in the city."

I reply, "It's easy to do when your niche is family portraits."

There was silence for a moment and then Knox posed a question, "I understand you took over the business from your father?"

I nod with pride. "And he was given the reigns from his father, who started the business in Harlem New York."

Leland said, "It's surprising that you have so much repeat business."

"Surprising to whom?" I snapped back without thinking.

Clearly the Director didn't appreciate my flippant remark. "Obviously, to those of us who requested this meeting."

"No disrespect intended Mr. Knox. Our business spans three generations, so quite naturally we're not surprised that the sons and daughters of the grandparents and parents of those we've photographed are our clients as well."

Knox's tone does not soften. "That's all well and good, but typically photography studios generate ten percent of your revenue."

"I don't know about other studios. We've built trusting relationships."

Knox smirks at me, "That trust certainly provides ample income."

"People will pay a premium to keep destiny at bay."

Knox's steely glare is unnerving. He barked, "What does that mean?"

I try to maintain my composure and come up with something to say without saying too much. "Custom Memories' portraits temporarily hold life still and our clients appreciate it."

Knox swings his head around to look at Agent Brewer. Directing his comment to him, Knox said "Leland, isn't a photograph a photograph?" Leland is uneasy and manages an affirmative nod. The director asks him "Is that a yes?"

"Yes, boss. A photograph is a photograph," Leland said.

"Then what is she babbling on about?"

Leland furrows his forehead, he's speechless. But I wasn't. Knox has just pushed me to my limit. We had not even begun to talk about the real reason why I was called into this IRS office, but it's too late today. I said, "You are quite rude Director Knox." I push away from the table and prepare to leave.

"You will be notified of the date of your audit, Ms. Grant."

"Really, is an audit necessary?"

"Clearly we speak different languages. I suggest you bring someone who can interpret for"----

Leland found his backbone and cuts Knox off. "--The audit will be scheduled in a few weeks. You will be notified of the exact date via mail. Thanks for coming in today Ms. Grant." He quickly escorts me out of the office.

Leland pivots around and stumbles backwards. Knox now stands toe-to-toe with him and said, "Who do you work for agent Brewer?"

The agent is perplexed with the question, but responds with respect. "I work for you, sir."

"Try that again and you won't. Don't you ever cut me off when I'm speaking."

"Sorry boss, I didn't mean to be insubordinate, but you were talking to her as if she's guilty of something."

"She is. Our job is to find out what?"

Knox's secretary, Stephanie, is as warm and bubbly as he is stoic and compassionless. She enters the office and greets Leland as he exits. "Director Charles, it's time for the retirement festivities. The staff is assembled in the break room. They're waiting for you."

His face reflects his usual disinterest, "Remind me again, in honor of who are we stopping work to celebrate during work hours?"

Stephanie walks over to the paper calendar on his bulletin board and points to a name circled in red marker. "Sir, it's right here in this bold red ink, big as day, Bruce Bamberger. You know the longest serving agent in the bureau."

Knox says, "Yes, of course, Bruce. Nevertheless, you all should proceed without me. I have too much to do here. I'm sure I won't be missed."

His response would be laughable if it weren't so cold and indifferent. Stephanie thinks to herself, "I hope this dude is gone before it's my time for retirement." But she remarks out loud, "Boss, you are the Director of the Department. Your absence will most certainly be obvious."

Knox couldn't care less and said as much, "I'll bid him farewell at the official agency ceremony. I don't need to say good-bye twice."

Stephanie is not surprised by his aloofness and indifference. She simply nods and walks away.

At the end of the work-day Knox leaves the office and walks to a nearby watering hole, Drakes Bar. The place is standing room only. Crowded with mostly men in business suites, Knox doesn't see an empty seat and saddles up as close as he can to a corner of the bar. He waits to be acknowledged by the bartender. Eventually, the two of them make eye contact and without exchanging words the bartender brings Knox a cognac on the rocks. Knox empties the glass and the bartender gives him another shot.

That night, Knox still wearing his work clothes sits alone in a darkened room in front of the television and falls asleep.

✦ ✦ ✦

Earlier during the day, Hanna guides IRS Agent Leland Brewer on a tour of Custom Memories Studio. As they walk through the atrium area, Zeph appears from the opposite direction and nods hello as he approaches. Hanna stops walking and directs her comments to Zeph, "I didn't know you were here already."

"Cameron and I need to touch up the paint in the Moments Room. I'm headed there now, but I see you don't need a touch up, still pretty as ever." He winks at her, looks Leland up and down and continues on his way.

Hanna escorts Leland into the DAY IN THE LIFE studio room. There is a large, framed photograph of fifty-seven legendary jazz musicians hanging on a wall. Its' engraved caption reads: A GREAT DAY IN HARLEM – 1958. Leland examines the photograph up close.

Hanna offers Leland a more vivid description of what he's reading. "This room was named in honor of that day in Harlem and reflects its' importance to the Grant family."

"Is that right?"

Hanna joins him at the photo to single out one of the children perched curb-side in front of the musicians. "This little boy is my boss's grandfather, Gavin Grant Senior."

"Is his father one of the musicians standing behind the children?"

Hanna shakes her head. "Gavin Senior's mentor, Victor Van Pelt, brought him along to watch the Esquire magazine's photo session, and her grandfather soon found his way into the shot."

"I've seen this photo before, it hung in my grandfather's home for years.   I didn't know that there was a connection to the Grants".

"I bet you also didn't know that this was the day that the seed was planted for the founding of the family photography business," said Hanna, proud that she can share the rich history associated with the company's beginnings.

"It's all very interesting; I appreciate hearing how everything interconnects. Thank you for the tour."

"You're welcome Mr. Brewer. Should I schedule a portrait consultation for you with Ms. Grant?"

Leland Brewer is headed out the door. He replied, "No not yet. I'll let you know when my family and I are ready for a sitting."

Hanna thanks him for stopping in and returns to the receptionist's counter. She busies herself scheduling previously confirmed portrait sessions and suddenly remembers that she has to deliver Ms. Grant's letter to Zeph. She finds him talking to Cameron and painting wall moldings in the Moments room just as he indicated. She approaches Zeph, "Ms. Grant asked that I give you this."

Hanna hands Zeph the envelope and quickly exits as he rips it open and begins to read. His face instantly tightens and it doesn't go unnoticed by Cameron. "Is everything alright?" the young man inquires.

"It will be. I want you to find out something for me." Zeph said as he reached in his pocket.

"Sure boss, what do you need?"

Zeph hands Cameron a few twenty dollar bills and replied, "I need you to go to lunch, and take Hanna with you."

A few hours later, Cameron and Hanna are at the Taco Joint Cafe. They sit outside underneath a large opened table-umbrella printed with hot chili peppers and margarita graphics. All the other table umbrellas are in a closed position. A waitress arrives and places tacos in front of them.

Hanna looks up at the umbrella and smiles at Cameron. "Thanks for opening it. I didn't think to put on sunscreen this morning."

"You live in the sunshine state. Plus your beautiful black skin doesn't need sunscreen."

"That's Florida, this is the Golden State."

Cameron simply shrugs his shoulders and takes a bite of his taco.

"A veggie taco would be better for you than the pork you're eating."

He's annoyed with her remarks and starts to think to himself maybe she's not as beautiful as he thought. Frowning at her, he said "Can I go with my own taste buds, please?"

She nods, smiles and changes the topic. "So you think Zeph's going to teach ballroom dancing full time now?"

"Damn, sure he doesn't' have a clue what he's going to do. He was just fired today."

"I know that, but it would be a no brainer. I used to take a dance class in his place. Didn't know him then, but It's a nice facility. Maybe he can use the space for Zuma or Yoga classes along with dancing."

Talking to her boggles Cameron's mind, he's not interested in this topic either and shrugs his shoulders for what seems like the longest time. "What's up with the dude who toured the studio today?"

It's Hanna's turn to shrug. "What do you mean what's up? That's my job, that's what I do, show people around the studio and schedule portraits."

"Yeah but, I caught a glimpse of the dude. He looked official like FBI."

"He looked like a regular man to me. He said his name was Brewer and he works for Internal Revenue."

Cameron is surprised "Wow, that's worse than the FBI. Is the studio in tax trouble?"

"He wasn't here on official business, checking out local photographers to take a family portrait."

Nothing else to ask her about the mysterious dude that piqued Zeph's interest, at least Cameron couldn't think of anything. He glances at Hanna drinking from her water glass, and gulps down the rest of his cocktail. "Why am I drinking margaritas by myself?"

"I'm going back to work, I can't drink."

"What about after working hours, do you drink then?"

While the two of them attempt to discover each other through conversation that could hold their interest, Zeph sits at Gisele's desk rummaging through her files and searching computer records.

Later that evening Zeph nurses a beer at Vancleef's, a local Oakland bar. He spots Cameron searching for him and waves. "Hey man, you want a beer?" Zeph inquired of his former protégé. Cameron nods. Zeph speaks to the barmaid, "Another cold one for my friend here."

The barmaid looks Cameron over and said, "Let me see your ID honey." Cameron hands her his driver's license.

She examines his license and pronounces rather loudly, "I wouldn't have bet you were a day over sixteen, twenty-five huh?"

Zeph laughs. Cameron groans and responds, "That explains why the ladies won't give me the time of day."

She places a beer in front of Cameron, rubs her palm across his hand and winks. "Some of us like men who look young, and are young." She chuckles and turns to direct her attention at another customer.

Zeph checks out the barmaid's backside as she talks to another customer and turns back to Cameron. "That chick wants you. She's old but may be able to teach you a thing or two, if interested."

Cameron shakes his head, "nah, I travel in the non-cougar zone."

"Whatever floats your boat. Did you find out anything?"

Cameron slides money across the bar-top towards Zeph. "The man's name is Brewer and he works for the Internal Revenue. He was only there for personal reasons."

"Why are you sliding that over here? What do you mean personal reasons?"

"It's your change from lunch."

Zeph pushes the money back towards Cameron. "I can't do nothing with chump-change. Keep it."

"Dude was looking for a family photographer," Cameron said.

Zeph smirks at the response. "That's how the government plays it now?" Zeph is quiet for a few minutes. Then he says, "Do one more thing for me? I need something else from the studio."

"Sure, what you need? I'll bring it to you tomorrow after work."

Zeph looks in the direction of Cameron but he doesn't see the young man. The rage from deep within Zeph's soul escapes through his steely glare and he bellows, "Now, not tomorrow. This has to be done tonight."

Within an hour Cameron is back at the photography studio. He's in a storage room. Several rows of cardboard boxes fill the metal shelving in the room while racks of cylinder canisters occupy most of the floor space. He searches around the shelves in vain. Out of frustration he dials a number into his cell phone. Zephs' voice comes through the speaker before Cameron has a chance to utter a word, "You have it?"

"There's like a million boxes in here."

"Have you looked in the tubes on the floor? I told you it would be stored in one of those."

Cameron walks over to the canisters and locates the one he was sent to retrieve. "Okay Zeph, I got it." Ending the call with Zeph, Cameron sends a text. It reads, "Meet me at VanCleef's in an hour, I owe you a Margarita."

Returning to the popular neighborhood watering hole, Cameron finds Zeph in the identical spot at the bar, guzzling down beer, with the same expression of rage on his face. He hands Zeph the canister. "You look like you could kill somebody. What's inside the canister?"

Zeph's angry eyes could burn through Cameron. "What's with your questions?" Cameron begins to bite on his lower lip. He looks sheepish. Zeph softens up. "Thanks for picking it up for me Cam. This delivery successfully concludes our working relationship."

"What are you going to do now boss, I mean Zeph?"

Zeph looks around the bar and chuckles. "I'm going to sign up some of these chicks for dance lessons." He jumps off the bar stool and approaches a table full of laughing females.

Cameron raises his hand to signal the bartender. Hanna slides in behind and startles him when she whispers in his ear. "This is where you wanted to take me on our first date?"

"I didn't see you come in, and technically, lunch was our first date," Cameron said.

Hanna glances down and notices the Custom Memories labeled canister propped up on the floor underneath the chair.

Cameron continues, "What can I get you to drink?"

Hanna glances around the room and spots Zeph speaking with three thirsty looking women. She gestures in Zeph's direction before responding to Cameron. "I handed him termination papers this morning. I'd rather not have to try and think up chit chat with him tonight. If it's okay with you, can we go someplace else?"

"Sure, fine with me," Cameron said as he stepped away from the bar and started to walk towards the door.

Hanna looks at the photography studio's canister leaning under the chair and said, "Don't forget that."

Cameron replied, "I picked that up for Zeph, it's his."

The young couple walked to Sends' restaurant and sat at the bar. Cameron ordered a beer for himself and a lemon drop for Hanna.

"So how do you like working at the studio," she asks Cameron.

"I love it. Zeph was hard to please but he's taught me a lot. I'm saving up to buy a house and needed to know how to fix stuff and paint. He's the best handy-man around."

"Buy a house? You must have a lot of money saved. I'm still

living at my parents place, and it's an apartment. Who can afford to buy a place in this area?"

Cameron responded with a cocky self assuredness, "You know how big this country is, who said I have to buy a house in California?" Then he asked, "Have you always wanted to work for a photographer, or is this job a stepping stone?"

"I want to model, do runway work in Paris and stills for magazines. I figured Ms. Grant will eventually show me how to pose and carry myself so that the big name fashion designers will come calling."

"Well you're pretty enough to be a model. But I don't know if designers will come looking for you. You're going to have to go after the work, get your face out there."

"Yeah you're right. I'm going to ask Ms. Grant to photograph me, so I have glossies to start sending around. I need her to like me first."

Cameron is bewildered by Hanna's comment. "You say the weirdest things. What does liking you have to do with snapping your photo?"

With an innocence and charm that matches her youth,

Hanna replied, "if she likes me, I'll be more relaxed in front of the camera and my photos will be better. I won't be able to afford any do-overs. The headshots will have to look good the first time."

Cameron might not understand her thought patterns, but he certainly was smitten. He looked at her lips while she spoke, and didn't necessarily hear her reply. He asked, "Do you have a boyfriend?"

CHAPTER 13

HE RETURNED HOME SOONER THAN EXPECTED

✦

I'm sitting in the dining room sorting through black and white photographs spread over the table-top. There are two separate images in the photos - a female teenager hanging out in a park and the other is of a young man spraying graffiti on a wall alongside train tracks. My father arrives home and joins me.

"Hi daddy, you're looking good."

Gavin smiles and puffs out his chest. "Thanks baby, sharpness is next to Godliness."

"It's cleanliness, Dad."

"Don't they go together? What am I missing?"

Talking to my father can be amusing at times; all I can do is gently roll my eyes and chuckle. Dad pride fully remarks on the teenager's photographs I've been examining, "I shot those this morning."

I hold up one of the photographs of the young girl, "You know she's pregnant right?"

"Why would you say that?"

"Maybe it's because, I'm looking at her baby-belly in this photo."

My father looks closer at the photograph and said, "Obviously, she's out then."

"You need to be able to see them Dad, if you're going to select the right time-travel candidates." He responded with a quote from the bible.

"The good book says days go by and every vision comes to nothing."

I don't want to be disrespectful and quickly stifle my desire to laugh. Sometimes his attempt to fit Bible quotes into a situation is a real stretch. This time, it's easier for him to link the Bible to his failing eyesight than to admit that he's reluctant to wear his glasses. "I understand that Dad, but where are your bifocals? You have to wear them if you're going to see through the camera lens."

He shrugs, interrupts me and picks up one of the photos of the graffiti artists. "Do you at least recognize this young man?"

"Should I?"

"Look who needs glasses now."

I stare at the photo for a few more moments, but I have to admit the person doesn't look familiar.

Dad said, "He's taller and more muscular now, but that's William Johnson."

I look again and am surprised at the sadness and hopelessness that comes through the photo. "Is that Roger's boy? I remember the last time I saw the kid he was full of life and light. I thought he was away on a basketball scholarship?"

"He returned home sooner than anyone expected."

"Why, what happened?"

"Roger indicated he couldn't focus his attention away from his mother's death?"

"So he quit?"

"I guess you can say that. He wouldn't practice, didn't study. He just gave up, so the school asked him to leave."

"From the looks of this photo, he spends his time smoking weed and spray painting walls." I hand the photo over to my dad. No relatable bible quotes this time.

He's pretty sullen, "You got it right sweetheart."

"Do you have any ideas how to get him into the studio?"

Dad looks at me like he's waiting for an apology and said, "What do you think?"

I actually did apologize and admitted that I have faith in him, even if in this situation, it is the size of a mustard seed.

A few days later Dad sits in a modest apartment. It's tidy but dusty and would benefit from a woman's touch. He sits opposite Roger Johnson and his son William. Roger is smart, but clearly doesn't give a damn about the use of correct grammar. He's also a no-nonsense type personality, who is prone to illogical rationalizations. William looks pretty much as he was reflected in Dad's photographs, inattentive and withdrawn.

Dad directed his comments to the young man, "The tribute takes place in Civic Plaza. Will you come?"

William squirms, he's not interested. "I don't think I can make that."

"The coach only agreed to it if we rounded-up the whole team," Dad replied.

"Boy, have you forgot all the support he done gave you?"

William continues to fidget in his chair. "How could I forget?"

"The same damn way you forgot everything else you posed to be doing," Roger barks at his son.

The tension between the two quickly went from zero to one hundred. The rage between them startled my father when William, visibly upset, jumps up with such force he knocks over a floor-lamp. He's fuming and stands with clenched fists.

William said, "On a serious note, are you serious? I mean seriously, since when do you care?"

His father rises and stands toe to toe with his son, so close that they're breathing the same hot air.

"Roger, listen to me. This is not the time," my dad said as he stands between the two raging men.

William moves away and picks the lamp up off the floor that he knocked over. "If I do anything less than perfect, he's Johnny on the spot to criticize. He doesn't give a damn about me, only mom was in my corner."

"Don't disrespect me boy. You ain't the only one lost without mom. Now I got to sit and chit-chat on things she would handle."

"That's my point, I'm just a thing to you. Your credibility game just went to zero."

Roger is irritated and ready to pounce on his son. Gavin guides him over to a chair and Roger reluctantly plops down. Gavin walks over to William and places an arm around his shoulder. "Son, you need to honor your mother and your father." He turns the young man to block the vision of his dad. "If you think attending the tribute for Coach will be too much for you, just come to the reception afterwards."

"Where is it going to be?"

"In the lobby of the Custom Memories studio, you remember where we're located?"

William nods.

"You can leave after the group photo, okay?"

William's face is blank. He simply shrugs his shoulders and says, "I can't make you any promises."

CHAPTER 14

THEY'RE CALLED PORTRAITS

✦

When I drove my sports car into the driveway, I waved at my father in the side yard attempting to trim tree branches with an extended pole pruner. He waved back at me but doesn't stop pruning.

I climbed out of the car and yelled over to him, "We can hire people to do that you know."

"Uh-huh I know, but let me have some fun, alright?"

"Dad, I've been thinking that we need to share more of the wealth."

He finally pauses the pruning for a minute and looks at me. "That's a good thing. What do you have in mind?"

"Well you know there's a waiting list at the Day Care."

"Of course there's a waiting list, attendance is free."

"There's more than enough money, we should open centers in other parts of the city."

"The scripture says the more you help others, the more you will be helped. Sow as many seeds as you like baby-girl, just make sure ---"

I finish the sentence for him ---- "every child at every center has a camera," and give him the biggest hug. "Almost forgot to ask, how did it go with William?"

His voice softened and at the same time the tree-trimmer tool fell out of his hands. "It went," he said.

"Be careful Dad, that thing can cut you."

He grabs hold of the fallen tool and reaches for another overgrown branch.

I continued, forgetting that I should have faith in his persuasion abilities. "You realize that you don't make it sound very promising."

"It wasn't," he responded.

"You don't think he'll show up?"

"Suffering is not a reliable indicator, and he's deep into it."

Our conversation is disrupted by a waving and smiling Chuddy, as he pulls his SUV in the driveway behind my car and gently taps my bumper. He exits his vehicle carrying a cigar box. Dad puts the pruning shears down to greet him.

"Hey kid, how you doing?"

"Who are you calling Kid, Mr. Grant?" Chuddy extends his arms around him for a big bear hug.

Dad chuckles, "Hope those are the cigars I've been craving."

"Only if you're hungry for a Dominican blend, strong peppery taste, with a tobacco wrapper hand-rolled in Oaktown," Chuddy said, as he hands my father the cigar box.

"Did I say Kid? I meant to say, you're the man Chuddy D. Actually, you're my favorite man." The two of them laugh.

I decide it's long-past time for me to be acknowledged and sarcastically remarked, "Hello to you too Mr. Dunn. Thanks so much for the gift, you shouldn't have." Chuddy walks over and embraces me. A smile crosses my face and I'm thinking, being enfolded in his big strong arms is the best of gifts.

A little while later, Chuddy and I are in the house gazing out of the windows looking over the neatly groomed backyard.

There are several rose bushes lining the yard's edges and a children's swing-set is positioned in the middle. Chuddy said, "I can't believe that swing is still standing."

His remarks sent our thoughts back to the year 1987, Chuddy is eight, and I'm seven years old. In tears, I'm holding crumpled up photographs and sit motionless on the swing. Chuddy stands beside me and asks, "What's the matter?"

I hold my fist up, showing him the crumpled up photographs inside. I say, "I took these stupid pictures."

Chuddy attempts to smooth out the wrinkles so he can look at the photos. "These photos are beautiful. Why don't you like them?"

I began to explain my pain to Chuddy. Moments earlier I ran into the house with such excitement I could barely contain myself. I wanted to show Mom the rose photos I took with my own camera. Dad had just developed them for me. I stood inside the doorway screaming her name. Mommy entered the foyer and forcefully closed the door I'd absent-mindedly left ajar. "What have I told you about leaving the door open?"

I said, "Sorry," while attempting to hug her. Mommy steps aside to evade my reach.

"You know we don't do that, Gisele."

My exuberance is instantly depleted. Completely deflated, I stared at the floor and mumbled. "I just wanted a hug Mommy. Can I at least show you my photos?"

"Do you mean, May I show you my photos?"

"Sorry, I forgot. May I show them to you?" I hand her the photos and said, "These are my favorites."

My mother looked at the photos and said, "What am I looking at?"

I can't believe she can't tell what it is. With all the passion I can muster I mutter, "It's the roses from the backyard."

She scrunches up her face, looks at me as if I'm an idiot and says, "It's too blurry, looks like nothing."

Tears run down my cheeks.

That ends the story, but I'm still crying as I look over at Chuddy. He pokes out his lips like he just sucked on a lemon. "Stop crying already Gee."

I used the back of my hand to wipe my face. "Didn't you hear me? Mom said they look like crap."

"I told you they're nice, don't I always tell you the truth?"

I can feel something sliding down my nose. I take a big sniff because I don't want Chuddy to see my snot. I nod my head in response to his question.

He continues, "You took these pictures, and you like them right?"

I nod again.

"So what's the problem Gee?"

I simply shrug my shoulders. "You're my best friend Chud."

Chuddy walks over and wipes his sleeve across my tear-stained, snotty face and says, "Remember that, when you're famous taking pictures of the rich and famous."

"Portraits Chuddy, they're called portraits."

We both laughed until our stomach's hurt. Then Chuddy pushed me high on the swing and my crumpled up photos fall to the ground.

Dad's in the backyard now and makes his way towards the rose bushes. Seeing his body in our line of vision breaks the memory-lane walk Chuddy and I were on as we peered out the window looking at the swing set.

Chuddy announces he has to leave. He hugs me and darts out of the house towards his car in the driveway. He yells over to Dad who is walking from the backyard. "Mr. Grant, you can't improve on perfection."

Dad smiles, "You have a point there son. Leaving already?"

"She's feeling nostalgic. You know cranky is next, so I'm getting out of Dodge." Chuddy laughs. "I'm only joking. I have to run by the Chamber, I'll talk to you soon."

CHAPTER 15

WHY WEREN'T YOU BURNED?

✦

I'm sitting in the dimly lit study, sipping wine and looking through old photo albums. Dad stands in the doorway in silence for a few minutes, observing me. Then he said, "Why is it so dark in here?" He walks over and flips on a light switch and notices the photo albums are open on the pages holding pictures of my mother.

"I don't know why you married her; she was so cold - downright hateful."

He looked my way with the saddest of eyes. "Don't you ever think that way about your mother. What does Exodus 20:12 say?"

I look up in his direction, but I don't see him. My eyes are filled with both rage and sadness. I don't respond to his question, because I knew he would answer it himself. He paraphrased the bible quote, "Honor your mother so that your days may be long."

"How am I supposed to do that Dad? She hated me."

I can't stop the tears from falling down my face. Daddy tried to console me. "No she didn't. She loved us both so much that it devoured her."

"I don't understand."

"It's time you do." He takes a deep breath and began to unravel the mystery of my complicated mother. "We had been married for a few years when she was finally invited to work the runways during Paris Fashion week."

"Should I say yeah, or just clap?"

"Neither is appropriate, nor is your sarcasm," Dad replied. "Right before she was to leave for France, we discovered she was pregnant with you."

I said nothing, simply waited for him to continue talking so his voice would drown out the sound of my heart beat which seemed as if it would pop out of my chest.

"We were overjoyed with the news, but once the Paris designers were informed of your mother's pregnancy she was blackballed."

"Why? That doesn't make any sense, pregnancy is not terminal."

"No one wanted someone's mother strutting down their runway."

"Oh I get it, the trade-off sounds about right. No Paris fashion shows, no affection for me."

"None of it was intentional Gisele, your mother lost her way."

My rage subsides and compassion is taking its place. "But she worked plenty of fashion shows in San Francisco, and all over California and New York, why wasn't that enough?"

"Looking at you in those audiences, she was becoming herself again. She was happier than she'd been in a long time. Then the fire came."

My father couldn't rein in his tears. We cried together and embraced each other.

"Where were you? Why weren't you burned," I asked him.

Dad began his response by describing how beautiful my mother looked that day in nineteen hundred and eighty-seven. They were both in the DAY IN THE LIFE room and mom sparkled as she slid her hand across a mural of herself as a young twenty-something year old. She said, "I've never seen this picture of me."

"You looked so beautiful. I snapped it before finding the courage to introduce myself to you."

She kissed him passionately and softly whispered, "Do you know how much I love you?"

"It took me forever to find the nerve to speak to you because I didn't think you'd be interested. You're beautiful indeed, but your sweet spirit called to me."

"Is it still speaking to you babe?"

"Like sunshine speaks to flowers and keeps them alive."

"You're the sweet one. Let's toast to us, is there any champagne left?"

"I'm sure there is, I'll go get." Dad walks through the studio area of the house into the kitchen. He retrieves the champagne from the refrigerator. Fiddling with the bottle's cork, it pops off and the bubbly spills on the floor. He looks around for something to wipe up the mess.

Back in the DAY IN THE LIFE room, Mom continued to admire her wall-sized likeness, then closed her smiling eyes and rested her back on the mural. I quietly entered the room with the family's special heirloom – the time travel camera.

"This one won't be fuzzy Mommy, say cheese."

My mother Cozette, startled by my command, opens her eyes and screams, "No baby." She lunges toward me. It was too late. I clicked the camera while part of her body was still in front of the mural. Although she was in motion, sparks ignite and catch her body and mine. Mom scooped me up and tossed me out the door, right before her body was engulfed in a fireball.

Dad completes the story explaining why he wasn't burned in the fire like mommy and me. I stare at him in disbelief. Suddenly, the realization of my role in mother's fate hits me hard. I let out a blood-curdling squeal which depletes my last bit of energy. My scream fills the room, "I killed her?"

CHAPTER 16

GET SOME OF THAT SUMO LOVE

✦

The lobby of Custom Memories Photography studio is jam-packed. An assortment of liquor and non-alcoholic beverages line the marble Receptionist's counter top. Hanna looks beautiful and serves as the barmaid. Wait staff passed around bite-sized hors d'oeuvres to happy and talkative guest.

My charismatic father Gavin and a group of enthusiastic young men surround a boisterous, jovial and confident man with a big-belly laugh. He's known as Coach. William is not part of the revelry. He's leaning on a metal art sculpture behind a large plant and away from the young men's line of vision. Gavin directs his comments to the Coach, "About that speech, did you think you were at a national Sports Awards ceremony?"

The young men cup hands over their mouths attempting to muffle laughter. Coach tries to save face, "My boys know

preparation is key. The ESPY's may be calling me any minute."
The guys fist bump with Coach.

I noticed William alone in the corner and approached him.
"You certainly have grown. Good to see you."

"Thanks Ms. Grant."

He puffs out his chest to appear strong and in control, but
the lack of sparkle in his eyes betrays him. I reached over to hug
him. "Are you ready for the team photograph?"

We make our way towards the coach. William's former
teammates notice and began to shout zealous greetings.

One guy said, "Hey, it's WILL-I-AM- the man."

Another shouted, "If it isn't the power forward, himself."

The smallest of the guys harbors a pinch of jealousy
towards William. He chimed in with sarcasm. "He wasn't the only
one with game. I had game too, remember when ---"

William smiled and cuts off the sarcastic guy in mid-
sentence, "—Peanut, still conjuring up stories that only live in
your head?"

All of William's former basketball teammates laugh and

embrace him. William's eyes lock on Coach, his smile fades and he begins to bite on his lower lip. Providentially, Coach spoke first.

"Glad you're here son, wouldn't be a State Champ reunion without you."

Coach reaches out and grabs him in a big bear-hug. William's shoulders drop and he holds onto the coach for a long while, until my announcement disturbs his peace. I said, "Winners, its photo time, follow my Dad."

My father chimed in, "I taught her better. Everyone's a winner, all God's children are conquerors. What she meant to say was, State champs follow me."

I swatted the air in Dad's direction and gave him a lopsided - give me a break – kind of expression. Dad carried two basketballs and lead the way through the atrium. Coach and his former team follow close behind.

The group entered the studio's Moments Room which has been transformed to resemble a gym locker-room. Employees of the photography studio position the former teammates and their coach around a bench.

"Gavin, toss me a ball", said the Coach.

Gavin complies and looks expectantly at the Coach for a command of what to do with the second ball. The coach continued, "Throw that one to the team Captain."

Gavin throws the ball with a little punch behind it. The ball slams into William's chest and the young man beams. I snap pictures and capture joyous moments of the guys through my camera lens.

"You deserve recognition Coach. If ESPN doesn't call soon, I'll contact them on your behalf," my dad commented with sincerity.

"Forget about it Gav, my reward was teaching these boys and watching them mature into great young men."

William seems to have transformed. The reunion and good will is uplifting and is reflective in his demeanor and sparkling eyes.

The moment I snap the last photo, my dad looked my way and asked, "When should Coach expect the prints to be ready?"

Coach waves a hand of indifference at my father. "Whenever they are ready, you need to deliver them with the case of beer you still owe me."

Laughter erupts again. The guys all fist bump. Dad escorts the revelers out of the room. I call out to William who is last in line. "William, wait a minute. I want to talk to you."

"What's up Ms. Grant?"

"Nice to see you smiling and laughing, you looked like your old self today."

"It was surprising; I didn't expect to be smiling. It was real good being here."

"What are you doing with your time these days?"

William's physical change is instantaneous as his shoulders and head slump. His smile transforms into a deep scowl. Irritated, he snaps at me, "I have to go."

He starts to walk away from me and I grab his arm. "Let me show you something before you leave".

I guide him towards the Day In The Life room. I walk into the room and William stops at the doorway. His questioning eyes dart back and forth between the mural and me. The mural reflects a younger William on the high-school basketball court, shooting a lay-up. The eyes of Coach, his teammates and the gymnasium crowd are all on him.

"Come in William and lock the door behind you please."

William enters the room, closes the door but doesn't lock it. He hasn't taken his eyes off the wall.

"Why didn't you use this room for the team's pictures with the Coach, instead of the fake locker room?"

I walk past him to lock the door. "It's for your eyes only."

"Come again?"

"What do you see?"

He shrugs his shoulders, his facial expression tightens and he barks, "Same thing you do. What's going on Ms. Grant?"

"Bear with me for a few more minutes; just describe what you see for me."

He looks up and his face softens, "It was the last basket of the final game. We won, became State Champs."

"Tell me something else about that day, that time in your life."

As he remembers the emotions of that day, tears swell up in William's eyes. "Sumo jumped out of the stands in one second flat."

"Who is Sumo?"

"That's what I called Mom. Her hugs would squeeze the wind out of me."

Smiling and imagining the two of them in a warm embrace; I replied, "She loved you."

William looks at me. His eyes still moist, dart around like a caged animal. "What do you want? I need to get out of here."

"I'm trying to say that your mother wasn't just proud of your game winning shot."

An audible gust of wind gushes out of him. "No shit, Ms. Grant. Don't mean to be disrespectful, but tell me something I don't know."

"You first," I responded.

He shoots piercing daggers my way. Then, unexpectedly the moisture that had been filling his eye sockets finally let loose and the tears travelled down his cheeks. "My mother never missed my high school games. I hated playing college ball. No Sumo hugs, had to get out of there."

"I'm so sorry her death has been so hard for you."

I walk over to two chairs and a table where I've placed the family's special camera. I sit down and gesture for William to join me. He doesn't.

"Do you believe in second chances William?"

"No."

"Why don't you?"

"Bring my Mom back from the dead, and I will."

"I understand your profound disconnect. My mother died when I was seven."

"Then you know I'm sad half the time and angry the other half. I don't know what to do with myself."

"Honor your mother's memory by moving forward."

"Remembering anything about Mom, makes me hate everything and everybody that's not her."

"Will you let me help you?"

William is skeptical but perks up at the mention of some relief. His tears stop. "How can you help me? Help me do what?"

I tap the empty chair. "Sit down, I want to tell you a story."

William plops down alongside me.

"My grandfather started this photography business to be of service. Through that process he also discovered a way to time travel."

William listens to me in earnest, "What do you mean, time travel?"

"I can send you back to the time when you were chasing life, not hiding from it."

William looks at me, then cradles his head in the palms of his hands. He began to rock methodically and reacted with his familiar hostility and sarcasm. "Yeah okay, and my grandfather picked cotton for the sport and a desire to tone his six-pack."

His sarcasm is not surprising and suggested that I should try a different approach. "Listen to me William. If we snapped the original portrait of a time in your life that you were happy, we can send you back to that moment in the picture."

He glances over at his mural. "You want to send me back to the championship game?"

"You had a sense of direction then, felt real joy – right?"

"Will Mom be alive?"

I nod over to the mural, "Wasn't she in the stands?"

His face lights up and a wistful smile appears across his face. "Is it just like in that movie?"

I can't really disguise my bewilderment, my face tells him I don't have a clue what he's talking about. He continued, "You know, am I going to turn into a fly?"

Smiling, I shook my head, "You will still be you."

He fires off a succession of questions, each increasing his level of anxiety and disbelief. "This sounds crazy. Are you high? What does it cost? I don't have any money."

I need to calm him down and try to make my voice as soothing and as relaxing as I can. "It's your opportunity to start over, get back to who you were meant to be. It doesn't cost you anything."

He seemed to relax a bit. This time when he spoke, his

tone wasn't as anxious, "Travel to the past and then what?"

"Make better decisions for your life when you return." I hand him the smaller snapshot of the wall mural. "You must have this with you when it's time to come back to the present."

William examines the photograph and stuffs it inside his wallet. "I should talk to Pop about this."

I placed my hand on his shoulder and softly replied, "No one can know about this, not even your Father. If you want to do it, you have to do it now."

"Can Mom come back with me?"

"No. We can't bring back the dead, we simply help steer the living in the right direction."

William fakes a weak smile. Someone knocks on the door. I open it and my father walks through. "Hi Dad, we're just finishing."

"Then I'm right on time."

William turns ashen and suddenly bolts out the door. He barely makes it to the bathroom before vomiting. He rinses his mouth and pulls out his cell phone. He types a text: - POPS, SHE SAYS I'LL SEE MOM AGAIN. BE BACK SOON. I'LL DO BETTER, PROMISE. LOVE YOU MAN, and hits the send button. When he returns to the DAY IN THE LIFE room, Dad takes over where I left off.

"You must understand William, that you will only have twenty-four hours for your visit in the past. At the end of that time you must return."

"What happens if I take longer?"

"It's not an option son."

"So what is the point? What can I possibly do in one day?"

I jump in the conversation, "You will go back and let your Mom re-energize you in her loving Sumo way."

Dad furrows his forehead, "You two have your own language now?" he said.

"Something like that," William replied.

I want to make sure he's clear on what he needs to accomplish during his time-travel experience, and continued offering suggestions. "When you see your mother, talk to her about love and death and how to carry on."

William had difficulty understanding and did not hesitate to conceal his confusion. "What do you mean? She won't know she died, how do I talk to her about missing her?"

"You just talk to her about how she dealt with the loss of her own parents, and other loved ones. How she manages to be joyful and productive in spite of losing them. Listen to her and you'll know what to do when you return."

William relaxed. A wistful smile came across his face. "Just tell me why you picked me, why do you care?"

Dad replied, "It's hard to see your own value when your eyes are filled with loss and pain. But we see your value son, and will stick by you until you do."

William walks over to the mural and said, "Let's do this."

CHAPTER 17

I'M THE ONE WHO NEEDS HELP

✦

Gavin positions William flush against the mural. "Make sure you clutch the photograph to your chest when you're ready to return, and do it within twenty-four hours. Okay?"

William nods and Dad clicks the camera. The young man disappears.

In a second William is back on his High School basketball court playing in the State Championship game. The Bleachers are filled to capacity. The score is tied at one hundred. There are four seconds left on the shot clock. William releases the ball and it goes straight through the net. He made the winning shot and won the basketball game, 102-100.

An ebullient woman runs onto the floor and hugs William tightly around his neck. She is his mother, Evelyn Johnson.

William's voice sounds as if laughing gas had been pumped

into his throat, "Mom, mom, I can't breathe." Just as he removes his mother's arms from around his neck, his teammates swarm around him with delight. William's father and his Coach look on with pride.

A few hours later William and his parents are home in front of the television, watching LaHoya basketball. They are captivated by the game and confidently offer play-by-play analysis.

Evelyn Johnson remarked, "This team is not good under pressure."

"All of them are simply showboats. Ain't no sign of fundamental basketball anywhere," Roger Johnson replied to his wife.

Evelyn leans over and kissed his forehead, "Don't say ain't honey. That's why our boy is going to LaHoya. Those dudes desperately need his help." She squeezes her son tightly around his neck. William responds playfully. His voice sounds as if he sucked on a helium balloon, like it did after his championship game, when she grabbed him in the same manner.

"I'm the one who needs help."

His mother looks at William and quickly releases her grip.

He continued, "Sumo, you are the real definition of breathtaking."

The family laughs. Evelyn suddenly jumps up, grabs her purse and walks towards the front door. "I'll be right back."

William calls after her. "Where are you going? The game's not over."

"Just need a few things for dinner."

He hops off the sofa and races towards the front door. "Wait Mom, I'll go with you."

"No that's okay, finish watching the game. You can fill me in on what I missed."

Mr. Johnson chimed in, "You ain't missing anything but more show-boating." He rises from the sofa out of frustration at the ball playing, and walks into the kitchen to get a beer.

William's hand is on the front door knob. He opens the door for his mother and said, "I want to talk to you about a few things anyway."

The Johnsons live in a modest house on a block surrounded by other small, single family homes. Traffic on the street can only travel one-way. Evelyn is behind the steering wheel. She backs the family car out of the driveway down the quiet street. William, needing leg room, looks down and fumbles with the electrical buttons trying to adjust the seat backwards. Their Taurus sedan approaches a corner stop sign and Evelyn prepares to brake. William reacts as he sees some sort of light truck or Sport Utility Vehicle barreling toward them. He screamed, "Mom, get out of the way.

Evelyn tried to turn the steering wheel but reacted too slowly. The vehicle careened head-on into her Taurus. Evelyn and her son are crushed and die on impact.

CHAPTER 18

WHERE THE FAULT LIES

◆

It's early morning and at my request, Chuddy met me at the Oakland Farmer's Market. There are booths and tables showcasing fresh fruits, flowers, nuts, breads and assorted vegetables. The place is packed with customers. We stopped at a floral station and Chuddy contemplates which fresh cut flowers to select.

"I know, stay away from the roses."

"That's yesterday's news. You can pick them if you want; I use them in the studio all the time now. I even give rose charms to the kids in the photography workshop."

I picked out a few roses from the vendor's bucket and tossed them on top of Chuddy's pile. The vendor wrapped the flowers in newspaper. Chuddy paid for them and hands the bouquet to me. Then he said with a slight chuckle, "You finally realized it wasn't the fault of the roses that your Mom didn't like your photos?"

"Yeah, it was pretty silly of me huh?"

"No sillier than me thinking you started the fire on purpose because of her dislike."

I can't believe what he just said. Instantly I'm angry. I shouted at him, "What did you say?"

Chuddy looked at me; he's still chuckling and doesn't yet realize that I am furious. "I don't think that anymore, your father straightened me out a long time ago."

"You knew that I started the fire? Why haven't you ever mentioned it?"

My life-long friend finally gets that I am not in a chuckling mood. He replied: "Your father always advised me to stay clear of the topic. He said you were too fragile. He was right."

"Fragile? She was my mother, what the hell was I supposed to be, joyful?"

Chuddy doesn't know what to say. He refused to look my way and fixes his glance on the ground.

I remarked unpretentiously, "I never even knew how the fire started."

Well Chuddy clearly was startled by my comments and lit into me. "What are you saying? You've known since you clicked that camera. You just haven't wanted to face the facts that your mother died because of it."

"How many pseudo-shrinks do I have to listen to? You and your five-cent diagnosis can go to hell." I threw the just purchased flowers at him and stormed away, damn near running.

Chuddy is perplexed. He stood there watching my back and pulled a cigar from his shirt pocket. Rolling it above his top lip, he spoke softly to himself - "Guess I'm no longer invited to breakfast."

My father is disappointed when I tell him I'm not interested in cooking a full breakfast and Chuddy won't be joining us. All I could muster up the energy to do was to set out bagels, juice, coffee and a large fruit bowl. Dad began to read the newspaper and turned completely ashen. His hands trembled and his face looked grief stricken. He shrieked, "My God, my God."

"What's the matter Daddy?" Thinking he's having a heart attack or some medical emergency, within seconds I reached across the table to grab my cell phone and was about to dial 9-1-1.

He swatted the phone out of my hand and shakes his head. It was a struggle to find his voice, but he managed to say in a soft whisper, "They've always come back. This is my fault. I thought I could help him." He hands me the newspaper.

I glanced at the paper and saw a photo of William making the State Basketball Championship game winning point. Above his picture, the headline: MEMORIAL ESTABLISHED AT LOCATION OF HIGH SCHOOL STAR ATHLETE'S DEATH.

Dad and I embraced and let our tears flow.

CHAPTER 19

UNTIMELY DISAPPEARANCE

✦

Dad and I are in Custom Memories' DAY IN THE LIFE room. He stands in front of a wall mural. The mural reflects my dad as a young man standing next to his father wearing the pork-pie hat that Holland Shepherd gave him. I'm trying to talk sense into him. "You know Granddad can't bring William back."

"I made a mistake and picked the wrong kid. Who better to talk with about my mistake than my father?"

"Me."

"Gisele, you're wasting precious time. Click the camera already."

My father is stoic. He's holding a smaller photograph of the mural. He presses his back flush against the mural and nods at me. I look at him and turned away. I walked to a locked cabinet, opened it and placed the camera inside.

I said, "Granddad didn't create this travel portal for chit chat sessions. You and I need to figure out what to do next."

My dad can't conceal his pride in my hubris but he's pretty annoyed that I have disobeyed his directive. I tried another approach. "You've told me there was a person who didn't make it back under Granddad's watch."

He wasn't pleased to have to answer but he did so honestly, "More than one person through the years never returned under Dad's watch."

"Did he accept fault?"

My father blindly stares at me. His face is devoid of emotion, as if he's in a trance. "If they didn't make it back, then it was his fault. Just like losing William is on our hands. Maybe we should stop playing God."

Dad doesn't tolerate the perceived irreverence. My mention of the Lord snapped him out of his trance.

"Your mother and I didn't raise you to be sacrilegious. What does Deuteronomy thirty two-thirty nine say?"

I've already gone against what he asked me to do, when I refused to send him back to speak with granddad, so I wasn't about to ignore his question. Like a small child, I responded from memory, "There is no God besides me."

"Uh-huh, and what about Psalms one hundred forty three?"

I replied, "Teach me to do your will for you are my God."

Dad's returning to himself - the strong, capable and confident man he has always been. "We help people get out of their own way. Sometimes despite our good intention---

---"They're called home," I finished his statement.

"Exactly. Ecclesiastes reminds us there is a time to live and a time to die. Our camera creates something that's in between."

I'm glad to see Dad's back, thinking to myself that we'll now be able to figure out the next steps. I stared at him for a long time and remembered a key element to our time travel creation. "Didn't granddad refer to the in between space as an eternal suspension?"

"Yes, that's what it is, a real painful choice," he said. "Pain is difficult to face, we often shove it down deep but it always rises back to the top."

I need him to understand that action is necessary. I begin to pace back and forth. "Well Daddy, sticking our head in the sand is not an option. If the time traveler dies, someone must reap what was sown."

"You are right, either I must die; the last time-traveler prior to William will die; or the next traveler will be eternally suspended in time."

"How do we decide which option?"

The color drains out of Dad's face. He took a deep breath and responded, "Not lightly." Sitting down, he cradled his head and continued, "If I'm too slow figuring it out, the grim reaper will take the decision from me."

We gathered ourselves and left the studio. When we arrived home I whipped up a little something for our lunch. Neither one of us ate anything, nor did we look at each other. We sat for a period without speaking.

"We're not even considering any option that results in your death."

Dad looks at me, the sadness in his voice almost made me cry. "I can't see any other way."

"It's a good thing my vision is better than yours," I responded.

Leaving him sitting at the table, I walked into my bedroom. Staring into the mirror at my facial scars, I looked at the small photo of mother that was stuck in the mirror's corner. Tears poured out of me as I held up the photo and began to talk to mother. "I was so mad at you. Nothing I ever did was good enough. I just wanted you to disappear for awhile, I saw Daddy make people go away. I'm so sorry. I never meant for you to die. Now death is trying to claim Daddy. Pounding my fists in the air, I began to sob uncontrollably. I conclude my pleaful prayer with all the passion I could muster, "Please help me."

CHAPTER 20

I DIDN'T CATCH YOUR NAME

✦

Ramona and Edwin Day will soon be celebrating their twenty-fifth anniversary. My assistants have completed the studio room set up and positioning the couple in flattering poses. I am in the process of happily photographing them in warm and loving embraces. Ramona's travel back in time was a success. Her husband's current reverential and tender behavior towards her is the tangible proof.

A cell phone rings. Edwin pulls the phone from his suit-jacket pocket. He looks down at the phone and turns to his wife, "Sorry to interrupt baby, but I need to take this call from the office. I'll be back in a minute." He winks at her and vaults out of the room.

Ramona speaks to Gisele in soft tones so that the assistants in the room can't overhear. "You and your father are a Godsend to me. Everyday feels like a honeymoon. Thank you so much." She reaches out and hugs Gisele.

"You did all the work. It's wonderful to see the love restored."

"There is one other thing." Ramona looks sheepishly at Gisele and continued, "The Internal Revenue Bureau wants to talk to me about your services. How should I handle it?"

A few days later, Ramona sits in a small cluttered office across the desk from Internal Revenue Agent Leland Brewer. Leland jots down notes while Ramona, eyes bulging, shifts uncomfortably in the chair.

Leland thumbs through papers and poses a question, "Custom Memories has been your family's photographer for just over twenty years?"

"That is correct."

"Have you had family portraits taken by that photography studio each year?"

Ramona nods, "Yes."

"How many times have you paid them a million dollars for their service?"

"Once."

"Why was that time different than the others?"

Ramona proudly sits erect and with great confidence states, "They photographed our only child's wedding - our daughter, Kay." She slides a photograph over to him showing the joyful newlyweds flanked by a beaming Ramona and Edwin. "We expressed our appreciation for the wonderful job they did photographing this important occasion."

Leland looks at the photo, "You were extremely generous in your appreciation."

"We don't think so. In addition to the wedding ceremony and reception, Custom Memories also handled their engagement photographs. Not everyone could have captured the tenderheartedness and sheer joy reflected on all our faces. The work done by the studio is priceless."

The interrogation of Ramona comes to an end. Leland picks up the telephone receiver, dials and asks, "Is the Boss in?"

Leland is uncomfortable as his boss berates him, yet again. Knox said, "So you're telling me that the Hunts panned out. The payment was completely legitimate?"

Leland nods. "They're long-standing clients with money to burn. Each transaction with the Hunts was reported in tax filings by Custom Memories."

"How many of the photography studio customers paid a million dollars for their services this year?"

"Sixty."

"Then, why are you still here?", Knox barked.

Leland doesn't understand the question. He looks at his boss who has already dismissed him and is busying himself with paperwork. "Excuse me, Sir?"

Knox is inattentive to his employee and doesn't bother to look up at Leland. He simply remarked, "Go do your job. You have fifty-nine customers to interview."

Leland's days were full interviewing a variety of Custom Memories wealthy clients. They were not a monolithic group, the only similarities being their deep pockets and their fondness for the work of Gisele and her father. One client was a well-known African American A-list movie star who informed Leland that the photographers are the only ones contracted with to document his private parties and events. A Caucasian couple shows Leland copies of photographs of themselves hiking on Mount Tamalpias that were taken by Gisele who accompanied them on the expedition. Another couple, trying to quiet a set of infant twins shows him family portraits that were taken by Mr. Grant when they themselves were toddlers.

Leland found the stories fascinating and their business relationships with Custom Memories, though expensive, were all above board. No tax evasions to be found. He is about to leave work one evening when he is startled by the appearance of Zeph standing in the doorway carrying a large canister.

"You're Leland Brewer aren't you," Zeph asks.

"Have we met? You do look familiar."

Ignoring his question, Zeph hands the canister to Leland. "Here's a Custom Memories client that you won't find anywhere in their tax filings".

Leland pulls the rolled mural-portrait from the container, and said "Who is this, and what did you say your name was?"

"His name is Chuddy Dunn."

Leland studies the image for a long time. It is of a teenaged, tattooed, muscled-body Chuddy chomping on a stogie. A fierce looking bullmastiff canine sits by his side.

"I didn't catch your name," Leland said as he looked up just in time to see Zeph slithering out the door.

Leland turns to his computer and Googles the name - Chuddy Dunn. He clicks on the first article that pops up. It reads: Oakland Chamber of Commerce President Elect Chuddy Dunn, successful nightclub owner, concert promoter, and former gang leader, is installed."

In a few days, Chuddy, Knox and Leland exchange verbal barbs around a conference table in Knox's office. There is repulsion on Knox's face and cockiness on Chuddy's.

Knox was rude when he addressed Chuddy. "You seem like a man who would resent paying taxes. How does such a man become President of a reputable business group?"

Chuddy responds in-kind. "Silent as it's kept, business owners don't like throwing money away either. Just so obnoxious individuals shuffling papers around from nine-to-five are able to live off our dimes."

"You're a philosopher too? Do you have any thoughts on felony tax evasion and criminal conspiracy to defraud?"

"Nope, sure don't," Chuddy said.

"We here at the Internal Revenue Bureau have plenty of thoughts on the matter."

Chuddy took a deep breath and confidently replied, "What does this have to do with me?"

Leland slides two photographs across the table. One is the exterior façade of Custom Memories' building; the other reflects the interior of a jail cell. He said, "We understand you like photos, pick one."

Chuddy remained composed, but clearly is losing patience. "I'm not following."

Knox still smug, attempts to clarify. "If you select photo one, you're agreeing to sign an affidavit declaring Custom Memories is your shill. Otherwise you're indicating your preference for taking up residency in a facility like the one in photo two."

"That's nonsense. They're simply my lifelong photographer."

"Funny thing, they don't have invoices reflective of your transactions, even though you've been paying them a ton of money."

"We're family. They don't charge me but the family card should only be used sporadically, so I pay them a retainer."

Chuddy chuckles, Leland's lips curl up into a semblance of a smile. Knox's expression hardens. "Uh-huh, a seven figure retainer is hardly plausible."

Chuddy pulls a cigar from his breast pocket. "Your disapproval is not my concern." He slides the cigar into his mouth and pats his pockets searching for a lighter.

"You can't smoke in here," Leland said.

Chuddy stands up; the unlit stogie dangles from his mouth. "I'm leaving anyway."

"You may want to concern yourself with these facts. We believe Custom Memories launders your money and both of you are under investigation."

CHAPTER 21

WHAT YOU GONNA DO?

✦

It's a beautiful sunny day in the Bay Area, perfect weather for Oakland's Annual Art and Wine Festival. Mardi Gras styled dancers perform on the main stage. Cameron and Hanna hold hands as they stroll by Art booths and Wine vendor stations. Cameron comes to an abrupt stop in front of a booth selling vintage posters. He holds up a black and white poster of the legendary icon, Lena Horne. "I have to get this for you," Cameron said in earnest to Hanna.

"She's beautiful, but who is it?"

Cameron looks at Hanna with an expression of disbelief. "Haven't you ever seen the movies: Stormy Weather or The Wiz?"

She shrugs, "No. I never even heard of them."

"Well I guess I have to help you catch up." Cameron responded, then turned and directed his attention to the

Art vendor. "Doesn't my friend look like she could be Lena's granddaughter?"

The dreadlocked, dashiki wearing vendor with a nose ring and arms full of tattoos, replied: "You mean she isn't?" The two guys chuckled. Hanna blushes. The vendor added, "That's an original print by Victor Van Pelt, the noted Harlem photographer. Have you guys ever heard of him?"

Hanna and Cameron looked at each other and exchanged a knowing smile. Cameron quickly makes the purchase.

The vendor continued with his questions, "Have you two ever been to the Parkway Theatre over on 24th Street?" Hanna shakes her head. Cameron indicates he's been there. Directing his comments to Cameron, he says, "Why don't you take your pretty lady to the place this afternoon? Its classic movie weekend, guess what's playing?"

Cameron says, "Don't tell us it's Stormy Weather?" Hanna spontaneously covers her mouth and giggles.

Watching the movie screen comfortably from one of the Parkway's cushy sofas, Hanna is mesmerized as she listens to the beautiful Lena Horne sing the title song.

Hanna whispers to Cameron, "She's absolutely stunning."

He sweetly replies, "And you're a younger version of the lady." Hanna, smiling happily, rests her head on Cameron's shoulder.

While Cameron and Hanna enjoy their festivities, Dad, Chuddy and I huddle around the kitchen table. "Apologies to you son, I never thought you'd be mixed up in our mess with the Internal Revenue."

"Gavin, at this point I'm not worried about the IRS, I'm more concerned about the three D's."

Dad and I both look at Chuddy with a puzzling expression. Neither of us has a clue as to what he's talking about. "Your daughter's daunting dog house. She's assigned me a space there and won't speak to me."

He has such a way with words that Dad and I both erupt in laughter. After Dad cracks up, he immediately bows his head. "Son, that's a bad place to be. Shall we pray on it?"

"That's not necessary Dad. I just thought he was my friend, but we both know that real friends don't keep secrets."

Now it's Chuddy's turn to laugh hard. He bellows, "Like hell we don't. Do I have to remind you of everything we've been through? If I'm not your friend, tell me who is?"

Dad breaks the rising tension, "Certainly not those boys in the IRS office."

The three of us exchange glances and chuckle. In that instance Chuddy and I both relaxed. Dad looked at Chuddy and continues, "Wonder where they got your name?"

Chuddy and I, as if on cue, burst out in song in splendid harmony. "Bad boys, bad boys, what you gonna do? What you gonna do when they come for you?"

Astonished, Dad remarked, "You two are still singing that tune?"

Chuddy began, "The words have real meaning now", I moaned and then zestfully cut him off.

"—Like they were meaningless when we started singing this song during the days you were running the streets, huh?" I said, and flippantly tapped him on the back of his head.

My cell phone rings. Hanna's name appears on the screen. I activate the speaker mode and gesture to Daddy and Chuddy to speak softly so I can hear her.

"Ms. Grant?"

"Yes Hanna, is everything okay?"

"I just received a weird telephone call. It freaked me out."

"Breathe Hanna, tell me who was the call from and what did they say?"

"The man on the phone wouldn't tell me who he was. He only said that the studio should get ready."

"Get ready for what?"

"A raid, the IRS is coming to seize our assets."

Dad, Chuddy and I exchange long glances. I remain silent.

The tension in Hanna's voice rose. "Ms. Grant, Ms. Grant are you still there? Hello?

"When? Did the caller say when?"

A short time later I'm in the Studio's DAY IN THE LIFE room to retrieve the family's heirloom. I push the wooden panel hidden in the wall and the door springs open to reveal a small, steel safe. I dial the code, reach in and grab hold of our special camera and cradle it in my arms through the building. Chuddy is in the parking lot waiting and helps me into his vehicle.

He starts the car and listens patiently as I voice frustration. "Your office at the Chamber is really not any safer than leaving the camera here in the studio."

"You're probably right, I know another place that'll work," he said as he made a quick right turn at the corner.

After what seemed like an eternity but in actuality was only fifteen minutes, Chuddy exits from the California Cigar Corporation and walks briskly over to me on the passenger side of his vehicle. I said, "That took forever, any problems?"

"We have ninety-nine problems, but protecting your family treasure isn't one of them." He leans into the window and kissed me on the cheek. Then he placed a silver key ring shaped like a cigar into my palm. There are two keys attached. One of them has a number etched on the front.

"What's this?"

"The key with the number opens a locker inside the refrigerated cigar room that now contains your camera. The other one opens the rear door to this building so you can come back when you need to, after or before opening hours."

"I assume this place is owned by a Chamber member?"

Chuddy nods. "He's also a good friend of mine, and was happy to give me the keys. No questions were asked."

"You can charm anyone into doing anything you want, always have."

He looked at me, his bravado vanished and said, "I don't know about that. I can think of two people off the top of my head that don't fit that bill."

"Like who for example?"

He said, "Knox for one, and you for two." Then he leaned further into the window and kissed me passionately on the lips.

I loved that he kissed me but am beyond surprised. I don't know what to say. The safe route was to put the attention back onto Knox. So of course, that's what I did when I remarked that, "Knox is first on that ninety-nine list."

"I'm not a part of the street life anymore, but I still know people who are. One of them owns a bar that Knox hits every day after work. I make a call and Mr. IRS gets his ass kicked."

"That solves what exactly?"

Chuddy winks and replied, "It simply answers the question."

I'm clueless for a second, and then I start to giggle like a school girl. We began to sing in unison, "Bad boys, bad boys, what you gonna do? What you gonna do when they come for you?"

Chuddy walks around the vehicle to the drivers' side and climbs in. My longing gaze follows him every step of the way. I instinctively lift my fingers to my lips. Chuddy says, "Nice kiss, wasn't it?"

It was more than nice; I waited my whole life for his kiss. I tried to speak and say something sweet, but only, "Uh-huh, but why now?" came out.

"I wanted to do it nineteen years ago when I was afraid I'd never see you again. You know, right before your Dad sent me back to 1999."

Pretty shocked to hear his admission, I said rather sarcastically, "Obviously your desire wasn't too strong since you didn't do it." I really need to learn to muzzle my sarcasm; it's another defense mechanisms that clearly doesn't serve my best interest. Thankfully, Chuddy overlooks my wise cracking comment and continues to reveal his true feelings.

He looked at me in silence for a few moments and carefully selected his words. "Your father believed in me when no one else did. He wanted to help me get my life together. You were both in the room on that day, and I couldn't take the chance of disrespecting or disappointing him simply because I wanted to taste your sweet lips. You feel me?"

He leaned over and sucked on my bottom lip for a second, then turned the car on and drove me home.

As soon as Chuddy drove away, I jumped in my car and headed over to my best friend Gail's place. So much has happened these past few days and I needed to talk with her. We've been texting, but haven't been able to get together. I've never told her anything at all about the gift of time travel. No one, other than the travelers are privy to the family secrets. She does however, know everything about the rest of my life, and I wanted her feedback on what's been going on with Zeph and Chuddy.

Gail's a City Clerk by profession and is responsible for municipal elections and procedural documentations of City Council meetings. Needless to say, she has a no-nonsense, cut to the chase kind of personality. She's also very beautiful. Her beauty adds to her confidence and disarms most people. Even the pompous, self-assured elected officials she works with can't escape the allurement of her factual abruptness.

Gail opens the front door and greets me in her usual manner, "Wondering if I was going to ever see you again Missy." We embrace and I walk into the house.

"What're you talking about girl, we had dinner and drinks two weeks ago."

"Well I need another one right about now."

"What's up Gail", I asked. She was already filling two wine glasses before I got the three word question out.

She said, "Remember the last time we talked and I told you the former Mayor was filing a petition to place a measure on the ballot for the next election?" I looked her way, nodded and waited for the update. "Well she walked into my office with a small army of supporters and handed me a petition signed by ten thousand voters."

I took a sip from my glass and said, "That's a lot of signatures. So I guess you'll be putting it on the ballot. It was about prohibiting the sale of plastic bags and straws in the city right?"

"Right, but you guessed wrong." She takes a sip of wine. "I met with the City Attorney and the City Manager and was advised to return all ten thousand petitions to the chick. Apparently, they were in a non-conforming format."

"So you're going to give them back to her?"

"I already did."

I shrug, "Well, no love lost. She didn't like you when she was the Mayor, so now she likes you less."

"True. Now she hates me, and along with ten thousand of her closest friends is suing me. Claims I over stepped my role. My job is to accept the petitions, not analyze the content or format. Can you believe that?"

"Damn Gail, I came over hoping you would cheer me up."

She laughs. "I shall. I'm not worried about that hussy suing me. The City Attorney has that covered. On the positive side of things, my name will forever be on California legislation defining City Clerk duties once the ruling comes in." Gail struts around the table practicing her walk of fame. "Why do you need cheering up?"

"I told you I fired Zeph, right?"

She lifts her nose up in a gesture of righteousness, and says, "Never should have hired him in the first place. He was good with his hands at fixing shit, but I knew it was a matter of time before you two clashed. He's not the type that follows rules."

I wasn't surprised by her remarks. She's voiced strong opinions about Zeph several times, and was really annoyed with me when I started dancing with him at his studio. I reply, "What you don't know is that, he went to the IRS and led them to believe Chuddy and I were colluding to money launder."

Gail exclaimed, "Wow, talk about getting revenge for being fired. Dude goes straight for the jugular. What are you guys going to do?"

"Prove him wrong." I finish my wine and tell her that Chuddy finally kissed me, highlighting that it wasn't our usual sibling kind of peck.

Gail leans back in her chair and pops her eyes open wide with delight. She says, "Good, it's about time. I was beginning to think ChuddyD was gay." Then she jumps up and places what's left in the wine bottle into the refrigerator. She grabs her purse and shouts, "Let's go girl, we have shopping to do."

The look on my face tells her exactly what I think of her suggestion. "I don't feel like shopping, do you have to do that right this minute?"

Gail sighs in exasperation, and says, "What would you do without me? I don't need anything from the store; we're going because of what you need."

I remain silent and shoot her a quizzical expression.

She begins rattling off what she thinks I'm lacking, "You need a cute, silky little negligee'; some protection, and some Prosecco. Better yet, a nice blend of Remy Martin Champagne Cognac is probably more his style, you think?"

"Don't you think all that is a little premature? We only kissed."

Gail laughs. "Only you my friend would call a twenty year wait premature." She looks at her watch and says, "Stores close in two hours."

We jumped in her sports car and headed towards Richmond's Hilltop mall.

CHAPTER 22

THE ONE WITH THE FLAT-TOP HAT

✦

Hanna and I huddle on my living room sofa. I asked her over to explore if there were details missing from our phone conversation.

"Cameron doesn't know why Zeph wanted the mural," Hanna timidly replied to my question.

I'm a little incensed and regrettably, misdirected my bark at her, "But he stole it anyway and delivered it to Zeph, no questions asked?"

She replied stronger than I expected, "In his defense, he really didn't think Zeph was up to no good. Cam just figured whatever was inside the canister belonged to him, or was some task he needed to complete. Is he in trouble Ms. Grant?"

A soft smile spreads across my face, "He's Cam now?" Well that explains her strong defense of him I think to myself. Hanna blushes and looks embarrassed. I shake my head no to her question. But in reality, I haven't figured out if he was in trouble, yet. Cameron is the least of my problems. "Tell me more about Leland Brewer's tour of the studio."

She answered, "He was just searching for a photographer to take his family's portrait."

"He was looking for more than that."

Hanna's innocent little eyes widened. "Don't know if it means anything, but he did mention that his grandfather was friends with one of the musicians in the DAY IN THE LIFE photo."

Finally, we're getting somewhere I thought to myself, "Did he say which musician?"

Hanna nods. "I don't know the man's name, but it was the one with the flat-top hat."

My own eyes widened at that point. I don't believe in coincidences, but thanks to my father, I do believe in divine intervention. I tell her that "The hat style is known as Pork Pie, and the person wearing it was Holland Shepherd."

Later that night Dad walked into the study where I was thumbing through old photographs. He asked, "Did Hanna offer anything helpful?"

"Maybe, I don't know yet."

Dad looks over my shoulder, "What are you looking for?"

Not wanting to get his hopes up prematurely, I simply replied, "I have a hunch."

Dad reached down to examine some of the photos resting on my lap, up close and personal. Nothing he see's is familiar to him. "What is your hunch about?"

"It concerns an idea which will prevent you from leaving me before your time."

Daddy looked forlorn and tired. He paused to kiss me on my forehead and said, "When I go baby, it will be my time." He placed the photos back onto my lap and left the room.

I continued to look through photo albums and having no luck, I switched to my laptop and archived photos saved on the cloud. In an instant, I spot it. I jumped up and excitedly ran out of the room screaming for my father. I almost knocked him over in the hallway in my haste to deliver the good news. "I found it, Daddy."

His voice lacked any semblance of enthusiasm. There was a monotone of defeat in his response as he half-heartedly asked, "What did you find?"

"I found the Reaper's payment."

"Care to tell me what you mean?"

"I will, but I must call Chuddy first. He has to go pick up our camera.""

✦ ✦ ✦

Chuddy exits the cigar shop clutching the canvas bag containing our family's heirloom. He stops on the steps in front of the building and pulls out his cell phone to call me. "I'm holding it in my hands, are you going to tell me why?"

Not too long after I fill Chuddy in on my idea to resolve the IRS problem, Hanna is in the photography studio working at her desk behind the marble Receptionist counter. Suddenly, a half-dozen men burst into the studio wearing jackets emblazoned with IRS letters written on the back and brandishing weapons.

Hanna's face is flushed with fear. A man in a loose fitting business suit, sporting a military styled buzz haircut approaches Hanna and hands her a document. "We're IRS. That is a warrant to search the premises."

Hanna is beside herself with anxiety. She stammered, "But..my boss isn't here."

The IRS agent's face is made of stone; Hanna's obvious discomfort doesn't sway him to soften even the tiniest bit. His expression remains stoic as he replied, "She doesn't need to be." He gestures to his fellow agents and several men begin unplugging Hanna's computer and confiscating the contents of her desk drawers and file cabinet located underneath the countertop.

Hanna screeches at the men, "Can you please be careful? This countertop is marble". The agents pay her no mind and continue to bang into the shiny, expensive marble as they ravage through her workspace.

One by one, curious and unnerved, Cameron and the other studio employees enter the reception area. Cameron approaches Hanna and speaks softly, "Dudes are in the studio rooms grabbing cameras. Where is Ms. Grant?"

Another employee whispers, "What should we do?"

The staff was all so dumbfounded that they looked like lost children, sweating and too afraid to even move. Hanna gathers herself together enough to send me a text. It reads, "The IRS is here and they're taking everything."

I'm driving through the streets of Oakland when Hanna's text comes in. I pull the car over so that I can read it and respond. My response is short and sweet, "Text me the minute they're out."

She replied, "Okay"

Then it occurred to me that I should actually say a bit more. I send her a second text: "When they are gone, you and the staff take the rest of the day off. Lock up the studio behind you. I'll call you later." Then I select Dad's number on the dashboard of the car phone directory and talk into the speaker, "I'm on my way to pick you up, Chuddy is in the process of handling his part."

The IRS agents are no longer in the Custom Memories photography studio. The place is in disarray. It no longer resembles the upscale, polished space everyone is proud to be associated with and knows to be in immaculate order at all times. Hanna sends a text in compliance with my directive, notifying me of the agents' departure. She offers to stay and try to clean up the space. I decline Hanna's offer indicating it would be more efficient to simply hire a service. Hanna locks up the facility.

She and the rest of the photography studio's young staff gather in Emeryville at Minnie Bell's Soul Movement eatery in an attempt to recover from the stress brought on by the day's surprising activities. They enjoy the famous, scrumptious rosemary fried chicken and mouth watering moist cornbread, until Avery - Gisele's assistant, pulls out his cell phone. He displays photos and a video clip he snapped of the IRS agents removing computers and files from the studio. Avery asked, "Check these out. Do you think I should post them on Instagram?"

Cameron was first to respond, "Do you want to keep your job at the studio?"

Avery looked at Cameron and then Hanna and said, "Why would my job be in jeopardy?"

"Because telling the world that our boss's offices were raided would be wrong," Cameron said. He was becoming angrier the more he talked. "We don't even know why they were there, or what they were looking for. Use your head man."

Hanna chimed in, "I agree with Cameron. You could

destroy the company by posting these photos, and the video would probably go viral."

Cameron said, "I'm sure Ms. Grant and her father will fill us in on what's going on, they're good people." Without a glimmer of warmth, Cameron continued, "Just delete the photos dude".

Avery was taken aback by his coworkers' vehement distaste of his posting idea, so he simply tucked the phone into his pocket without deleting the matter under discussion.

CHAPTER 23

REMEMBER ME?

✦

It's the end of the work day for most and the streets in downtown Oakland are bustling with people on their way home. There is a "closed" sign on the door of Drakes Bar which is a very unusual situation for this time of day. Inside, the place is empty except for Chuddy and Bertrand, the bartender enjoying a cocktail. He was Bert to Chuddy ever since their teenage years, but Bertrand to everyone else.

Everything about Chuddy's countenance was serious and Bert quickly recognized the gravity of the situation. Chuddy asked him, "You're sure he comes here every day, the same time?"

"He's here every day at the same time, gulps down the same damn drink."

Chuddy sits up straight and looks his friend squarely in his eyes. "That's good man. As I told you on the phone, I need your help with a little problem."

"Anything man, you know that. Well - short of killing the dude."

Chuddy responded, "You know I ain't talking about killing nobody. Just keep the closed sign up until right before he would normally arrive. Immediately after he gets here, slip the closed sign back around, without him noticing."

"Sure, but why?"

"I need the place to be empty when you and I carry him out the back door", Chuddy replied in a monotonous tone as if he was talking about taking out garbage.

Bert replied with great sincerity, "No problem Chud. Only thing the bastard ever did for me was put liens on my place and hike up my fucking taxes. The funny thing is man, he comes in here every damn day and has no clue I'm the owner. Thinks I'm just the bartender. Son of a bitch, damn near bankrupted me."

The two long-time friends finish a second drink in silence. Each swallowing the distaste they have for Charles Knox. Chuddy breaks through the silence, "How are Bettina and the kids doing man?"

"They're good now. We're happy, but I almost lost them when the IRS came after me. They took everything to satisfy the liens. Bettina had to get a second job to help pay the mortgage on this place and the house. We didn't want to leave the kids unattended during the evening, so her mom had to watch them while we both burned the midnight oil."

Bert and Chuddy had been through a lot together when they were young men back in the day. A few years older than him, Bert always looked out for Chuddy as if they were blood brothers. "Damn man if you were that short on funds, why didn't you call me?"

Bert didn't think much of the question. He looked directly into his friends' eyes and spoke from his heart, "Because I would never be able to repay you. Why would I want to throw away our lifelong friendship for some bullshit?"

Chuddy tried not to show his disappointment, "It would not have been a loan man. I don't roll like that."

"But, I do. Anyway it worked out great, and it's going to be even better once the chump arrives." Bert said as he pours another round.

Chuddy holds up his glass, "Here's to friendship and family."

Bert clinks his glass against Chuddy's, "Love you man."

The men gulp down the shot. Chuddy climbs off the stool and walks behind the bar into the stock room. Bert pours a Cognac on the rocks for his regular customer and places it on the bar in front of the middle seat. Then he stands by the front door until he sees Knox walking toward the Bar and turns the closed sign around to open.

Knox enters and notices his drink poured and waiting. "Thanks man you have great bartending skills." He chuckles and looks over at Bertrand who is walking from behind the bar towards the front door, "Guess you can set your clock by me, huh?" Knox takes a swig. Bert swiftly turns the open sign over to closed, and silently locks the door.

Chuddy re-enters the bar area from the stock room and faces Knox. The IRS Director is surprised and afraid. He stammered "What the fuck is going on here?"

Chuddy was happy to clarify the situation for him, "It's your turn to be concerned. How you like it so far?"

Knox tried to rise up off the stool, but Chuddy reached

over and grabbed him. Chuddy covered Knox's face with a cloth doused in chloroform. Knox frantically pushed away from Chuddy but Bertrand is behind him and pinned down his arms, rendering any efforts to escape, useless. Knox quickly loses the battle and consciousness, his body goes limp. Chuddy and Bert hoist Knox up and placed his arms around their necks. They walked him around the bar, into the stock room and out the back door, which leads into an alley where Chuddy's car is parked.

Dad and I are in the studio's DAY IN THE LIFE room anxiously awaiting Chuddy's arrival. I have just completed posting a mural onto the wall and step down off the ladder. Two men pose with golf clubs on the greens of the City Country Club. One of the men pictured wears sunglasses and a baseball cap. Dad is staring at the mural with a blank expression. He can't quite figure out the identity of the man in the sunglasses.

"Can you help me out here?" Dad asked.

"I snapped it at a fund raiser over a decade ago."

Dad continued staring at the men and rubs his chin, "I recognize the former Mayor, but who is the other dude?"

Chuddy walked into the room with the answer to Dad's question. He has an unconscious Knox draped over his shoulder. Chuddy slides the IRS Director off his shoulder and props him on the floor in front of the mural. He said, "Delivered, per instructions Ma'am." He turns and walks back out of the room.

Daddy looks at me, "The one in the cap and sunglasses?"

I nod, "Soon to be the one floating between the past and the present."

Chuddy returns with a canvas bag and pulls out our family heirloom, the camera. He hands it to me.

Daddy is worried, "Are you sure no one saw you bring him here?"

"Remember me much Mr. Grant? Traveling Oaktown streets undetected is in my blood."

Vivid memories of the old Chuddy flash across my mind. "Hmmm" I said. "Knox is not the only one caught between yesterday and today." I shoot a knowing glance over to my father.

Chuddy said, "In this instance you both better be glad. Now can one of you tell me what's up?"

Director Knox moans, and the three of them turn attention towards the slumped over man on the floor. Dad said, "Hope he's not up anytime soon."

"No. He'll be out for a while. But explain to me what good is it sending him through time if it only last for twenty-four hours?"

I walked over to Chuddy and grinned. "The rule doesn't apply in this case."

Chuddy looks irritated. He mumbled, "Didn't know the rules were flexible."

Daddy jumped in, "They are when the time traveler didn't request the trip." Then my father looked me squarely in the eyes, "We've never transported anyone who wasn't able to agree with it."

My response was quick and sharp tongued, "Don't you think it's time? Obviously, Granddad did it once or twice himself."

"He never actually said that he took this path."

"The evidence is that Gramps lived a long life didn't he?"

My father's tone revealed that he's a bit annoyed with my insolence, "Meaning what Gisele?"

"Meaning it's not your time to go Daddy." I nod my head towards the slumped over Knox, "It's his." Without hesitation or regret, I walked over and stood in front of the IRS Director and clicked the camera. Chuddy sings, "What you gonna do, what you gonna do when they come for you?"

CHAPTER 24

THE GRANDFATHER CONNECTION

✦

Although Junius William's small law practice has only three staff attorneys, the firm has a stellar reputation of success. He is as shrewd as he is witty, and his understanding and comprehension of the law is remarkable.

He sits across a large cherry wood conference table from me, Dad, Chuddy and our accountant, John Watson. "No charges have been filed by the IRS against Custom Memories or against Mr. Dunn."

Chuddy chomps on an unlit cigar and is the first to respond to the lawyer's remarks, "No surprise there Junius, nothing illegal or underhanded took place."

Junius responded in his dignified, professional manner "Their investigation revealed all portrait fees and taxes were paid appropriately."

Daddy chimed in, "Watson here is on our payroll for a reason."

John Watson gives Dad a once over and only slightly in jest said, "About my fee Gavin, --"

---"Clearly it's not enough, since you continue to wear that ancient, moth ball smelling cashmere jacket," Daddy said. Everyone bursts out in laughter.

Junius turns serious. "Has anyone heard the news?"

"What news?" I asked.

"IRS Director Knox is missing."

"What do you mean missing?" replied Chuddy.

"No one has seen him since the raid on your studio."

Watson was the only one of us who appeared unnerved by Junius' announcement. He practically choked on his own saliva, "Damn, is that right?"

Junius is concerned, "Yeah man. You okay, need some water?"

Watson shook his head, tried to compose himself. "That's really odd, though. People just don't go missing."

"Guess you don't watch the news much huh? It happens every day, typically to children though," Chuddy said with a matter-of-fact tone to his response.

"Who's in charge at the IRS office?" Dad asked Junius.

A member of Junius' staff knocks on the conference room door and sticks his head in, "Sorry for the interruption boss, but I need to speak with you for a brief moment". Junius rises to leave and answers Dad's question on his way out of the conference room. "From what I understand, Leland Brewer has been temporarily appointed to fill the IRS spot."

Shortly after we all left Junius' office, I'm sitting in the visitors waiting area outside of the Bureau of Internal Revenue Service offices. The secretary to the Director is on the telephone announcing my presence.

I walked into the Office of the Director carrying a package and said, "Congratulations on your appointment."

Leland stood up, greeted me at the doorway, and responded with grace, "Thank you Ms. Grant. You didn't have to come all the way down here for that."

"I wanted to express my appreciation."

His face clouded over in confusion, "Appreciation?"

I handed him the package. He opened it to find an elegantly framed photo of musician Holland Shepherd in his trademark pork-pie hat standing between a middle-aged Caucasian man and a young Black man. A Broad smile washes over Leland's face, his eyes moisten.

"My grandfather and Holland " he remarked before I cut him off and said, "and my grandfather."

He's surprised and says, "My grandfather knew your grandfather?"

I shrugged my shoulders and lifted my hands towards the ceiling. "I don't believe they actually knew each other. My Gramps followed Holland around in awe whenever he could and snapped his photograph. Sometimes he would jump in the shot."

Leland chuckles. "Just like how they originally met on that Harlem curb, huh?"

I nod an acknowledgment.

"I've never even seen this photograph. How did you know this was my grandfather?"

"My receptionist indicated you told her he was a friend of the musician. So I checked our archives. It took me a minute to research the files, but then I saw the name – James Leland Brewer. He had to be your family."

We shared a warm, lingering smile. Then Leland walked over and removed a washed-out water color painting from the wall and replaced it with the photograph of our grandfathers. "Such a special gift, I can't thank you enough."

"Your tip about the raid of my studio was thanks enough."

Leland appeared surprised that I knew he made the call. "He was obsessed with bringing your studio down. Even to the point of framing your friend. Even though it was against all kinds of policy, you didn't deserve that injustice. I thought the least I could do was warn you."

"Thank you from my father and me. We have always understood that haters are going to hate, at least until due rewards comes looking for them."

He gives me a side-eye glance. "That sounds pretty ominous."

"I just believe that people receive what they give, and

sometimes it's returned with a vengeance."

"He's still missing you know, not a trace of what happened to him," Leland replied without any remorsefulness or accusatory tone.

"We heard that from our attorney, any leads from his family?"

"He wasn't very social around here, so our office can't offer police any help. As far as I know he's never been married and doesn't have any kids, so no family is even looking for him."

I shrug in indifference, and then remembered the other gift I brought for him. I slide a manila folder out of my tote bag and onto his desk.

"Sorry to hear about the dilemma surrounding your boss' whereabouts. Until he shows up, you may be interested in investigating a business with real and not concocted tax evasion issues."

His wide - eyed expression and his silence tell me he's listening. I continued, "That contains information associated with a local dance studio you may want to check out. If you make a site visit, word on the street is you may want to bring along drug sniffing Fido."

CHAPTER 25

APPRECIATION

✦

Later that evening I tried not to sound too giddy when Chuddy called to say we were going out to celebrate. He told me to put on something nice. I obliged and wore a form fitting cocktail dress with glittering rhinestones adorning its plunging neckline, and of course I was styling my favorite pair of strappy stilettos.

When we arrived at the elegant Pican's Soul Food restaurant situated in the middle of downtown Oakland, we were quickly escorted to a secluded, candle-lit table. Chuddy didn't allow the Maître'D to seat me, he preferred to pull out my chair himself.

Chuddy, about to sit, was stopped in the middle of his squat as the owner of the restaurant Paul Pican, grabbed his arm and began enthusiastically shaking his hand. "Mr. Dunn, I'm happy to see you dining in our establishment."

"It's the best food in Oakland." Turning to me, Chuddy remarks "Let me introduce you to Ms. Grant."

"We've known each other for years. Hi there Gisele, my apologies for not greeting you first. How's your father?"

"No apology needed. I'll tell Dad you said hello."

Chuddy always the ombudsperson said "Let me ask you a question, Paul."

"Sure, ask me anything."

"Are you a member of the Oakland Chamber of Commerce?"

Peter Pican, terrible at concealing his discomfort, diverts his eyes and tugs on his shirt cuffs. "I heard you were elected President, congratulations."

Chuddy reached inside his suit jacket and pulled out an index-sized card. "Here's a membership card. Fill it out and bring it with you to a meeting. I'll share some ideas for increasing your community visibility."

Surprised to hear Chuddy's interest in helping his business, Peter Pican accepts the card and gleefully replied, "For sure I'll see you there. You two enjoy your meal, it's on the house." He smiled at me and walked away to greet another guest. Chuddy finally sits and scoots his chair closer to me.

"I stopped by the IRS office to express appreciation for the tip-off."

He stares deep into my eyes and said, "Hope you weren't too beholden to the dude."

Blushing, I lightly swat the air, and since I never know the right thing to say to him I quickly changed the subject. "Well I wanted to pay Zeph back for providing your portrait and putting them on your trail. He'll soon find out he shouldn't have."

Chuddy is only half-listening; with his other half he's devouring me with those sexy eyes. "In case you haven't noticed, we're in a fancy five star restaurant. They don't really serve IRS here."

"Sorry, what do you want to talk about?"

"You look amazing. Why don't you wear clothes that fit like that more often?"

I smiled. "Thank you. You're quite the charmer tonight."

Now his voice had the same seductive quality as his eyes, "After all these years, you're just noticing my charm?"

We both giggled, and I managed to whisper, "Actually, Chuddy I noticed it when you liked my fuzzy, Rose photographs."

Chuddy shook his head from left to right and reached for my hand, "It was way before then. We charmed each other the first moment we met." He leaned over the table, palmed my chin and softly kissed me on the lips. Unfortunately my hair was in the way which prevented the kiss from being wonderful.

Much to my own surprise, I swiftly swept the hair away from my facial scars and pinned it behind my ear. I reached across the table for Chuddy's other hand and kissed him right back. This time we both smiled warmly at the emotions the kiss generated.

After dinner we stopped at Chuddy's place to retrieve the cell phone he'd mistakenly left behind. He walked from room to room searching for the phone while I waited patiently in the middle of the living room floor. Chuddy shouts from another room, "Call my phone number please."

I don't quite understand him and follow his mumbled voice into the bedroom. "What are you saying?"

He repeats his requests. I pull out my phone and dial. We hear the ring tone coming from underneath the neatly tucked-in bed covers. Chuddy pulls the King sized bed covers back to reveal his I-phone. Lying next to the phone is a single key, he chuckles. "Come here."

I walked closer and he wrapped his arms around my waist. "You know I'm not usually absentminded."

"You'll be okay. We have all been through a hell of a ride."

Chuddy began to trace my facial scars with his fingertips, followed gently by his mouth. He picked the key up off the mattress and slips it into my hand. "I'll be better when you put this on your ring with your other house keys."

With the warmth of his hands radiating on my hips, all my hesitancy and nervousness fell by the wayside. In that split second I decided it was time to express myself. "All these years, I've always wanted more from you than our sibling-type bond, but thought that was all it was ever going to be for you."

"It was, but that's no longer the case."

"Why did you change your mind?"

He looked at me and chose his words carefully. His voice was soft and there was a vulnerability about him. "Honestly, you were too good for me. You were beautiful, smart and going to attend college. I was a street punk doing what knuckleheads do. After traveling back in time, I've worked hard to build something for us and I'm ready now. You are my best friend. Use--"

I couldn't stop myself from kissing him hard which prevented him from completing his remarks. When I eventually released my hands from caressing his face, he continued - "Use the key whenever you want to be with me. I am yours."

"What happens if I never want to leave?"

Chuddy doesn't answer. Our eyes simply locked. Then he kissed my neck, sucked on my lips and laid me gently on the bed. We undressed each other. I grabbed onto his chest, played with his thick hairs, and licked and kissed his nipples. He fondled my breasts, suckled one and then the other. I attempted to pull the sheet up to cover our naked bodies but it quickly slid back onto the floor as I arched my back and moaned.

CHAPTER 26

WHY DO YOU THINK I PICKED HIM?

✦

There's a beautiful sunset over the San Francisco Bay. Dad likes to take a stroll through a West Oakland Park during this time of day. The view of the San Francisco cityscape, coupled with the vibrancy of the dropping sun over the sparkling waters, is breathtaking. Dad says walking this path was his and mother's favorite thing to do.

As we walk hand in hand, Dad's feeling emotive and temperamental. He looks my way with a strange expression and says, "Huge responsibility we inherited, huh baby girl?"

"I can't argue with you. How does the Bible quote go…uh, "Be strong and courageous, you will lead the people."

He interrupted me in an unexpected, melodramatic manner, "Which one of us is supposed to be Moses?"

"Granddad was more like Moses, you're sort of Joshua."

Dad stumbled on a pebble and loses his balance. He collected himself before he actually fell flat onto the ground. I feel old as Moses right about now."

"Come on Daddy, who hasn't tripped? You're not Methuselah."

He turned towards me and explained he was both delighted and humbled by how I handled Knox and the IRS. Then he surprised me by saying, "I don't know if my life should have been saved at William's expense."

"Neither of us knew William was so fragile. Your life wasn't tied to his death, Knox had that honor."

"I agree that the condescending dude sowed some things, but did they equate to what he reaped?"

"It's over now Dad, what are you getting at?"

"I'm afraid I've become a liability to you and Custom Memories. I'm making too many mistakes. Don't forget I also initially selected the pregnant girl.

I tried not to show him my disappointment with his remarks, but his defeatist attitude was really worrisome. "It worked out didn't it? William clearly didn't want a second chance. Besides, Granddad's vision can't continue without you."

Dad turned to me with a look of disappointment of his own. "You do realize I am going to die one day?"

"Come on Dad, aren't we all? I really think we should think about closing shop, I do not want to do this alone."

"What makes you think you'll be by yourself?"

I chuckled briefly, "I have a sibling that I don't know about? Without you, it's just me out here."

He smiled as he said, "You know there are no half brothers and sisters of yours floating around here. You also know that you're not alone."

"Are you talking about Chuddy?"

"Of course, I've been waiting on you two to get in step. Glad it finally happened."

Cheerfully I replied, "How do you know, clairvoyant now too daddy?"

Dad stopped walking and looked me squarely in my eyes. "He's always been a good guy at his core. Why do you think I picked him to time travel in the first place? Who better for you to partner with than someone who personally took the ride and is your lifelong friend?"

They share a huge smile and Gisele kisses her father's cheek. "I love you Daddy."

"I love you more, but I need to ask your opinion about something."

"What's going on?"

"John and Laura invited me to dinner; do you think I should go?"

His face says he isn't joking, he looks tense. "Why would you ask me that? Why wouldn't you go?"

"Laura's sister Lisa will be there. It seems she might be sweet on me after all these years."

I can't help but chuckle, at least this time I have the good sense to do it silently. "That's great dad. I don't remember you ever dating anyone, it's long past time."

"Are you going to help me?"

"You don't need my help, just go eat and be yourself."

He's still tense and sort of stammers. "Myself? Who am I? I

don't even know what to talk about with a woman. I mean other than you, but you're my daughter. You know what I mean?"

Clearly nervous at the prospect of keeping company, I can see that my dad is also excited about the opportunity. "If Ms. Lisa knows like I know, she's going to make sure you enjoy the dinner. You're the most handsome, stylish and captivating eligible man in this City. She's the one who should be fainthearted."

He grins. With a renewed air of pride he lifts up his chin a little more and thanks me with a wink.

CHAPTER 27

THIS PHOTO IS A KEEPER

◆

When the unmarked IRS and Sheriff cars pull up in the parking lot on the side of the Dance Studio their vehicles are quickly coated with the familiar white cement dust. Leland sits in a car parked directly across the street from the building's front door. He watches Zeph aggressively tug on the padlock draped across the door. While Zeph reads the neon green sign taped on the door, Leland dials the men sitting in the parking lot. "He's reading the notice. Come get him."

The notice on the door reads:

"NOTICE"

THIS PROPERTY LOCKED BY AUTHORITY OF THE SHERIFF.

Pursuant to the provisions of the California General Statutes and by order of the Sheriff of Alameda County, this property has been locked. Any person entering upon these premises without proper written authorization is subject to arrest as prescribed by the California Criminal Statutes.

The men exit the vehicles and walk around the building to Zeph, who at this point screams profanity as he is kicking the door.

" Zeph Williams?"

"Who the hell are you?"

Leland approaches and surprises Zeph, "Good Morning Zeph. Do you have any more murals you want me to check out?"

Zeph recognizes Leland but remains silent until one of the Sheriff deputies speaks, "We're from the County Sheriff and you're under arrest." A second officer handcuffs Zeph's hands behind his back.

"Why am I under arrest? I have my rights," Zeph barked.

One of the deputies responds abruptly, "Charges will be spelled out when we get you to the holding cell. That cabinet full of illegal substances will be on the list."

"As far as my agency is concerned, chief among your violations will be tax evasion and money laundering," Leland added.

Zeph is beyond angry, reminding all within earshot of his rights to speak to his lawyer.

◆ ◆ ◆

Back at the studio Robbie tidies up the Day Care and Children's Club. She stops to greet me when I arrive in the room with two little twin girls by my side. They survived a house fire last year and have small facial and forearm burns. Robbie finds seats for the children and I began the day's class.

"Everyone, please say hello to sisters Frankie and Billie. They will be joining our photography class."

The children shout in unison, "Hi Frankie, hi Billie."

"Before we share our stories let's recite the rules. What's rule number one?"

The children cheerfully respond, "My eyes are the best photography equipment."

"Number two?"

"I don't take a photograph, I make a photograph."

"Three?"

"Everything and everyone is photogenic."

Frankie and Billie's faces light up at the encouraging thought. I turn to see Troy fidgeting with his camera, and use the twins' delight as my motivation for what came next. "Troy, give Ms. Robbie your camera."

He's visibly alarmed that I called him out and pleads, "Sorry, I'll put it away. Please don't take it from me."

"No, no, I'm not going to take it from you. I want Ms. Robbie to use your camera to take a snapshot of all of us together."

Troy hesitates and looks confused, "I thought you said pictures of you are not allowed?"

I looked over to him, smiled warmly, and replied, "Did I?"

Troy shrugs his shoulders and presents his camera to the teacher. Robbie shepherds the children into positions around me to ensure we'll all fit into the frame. At that moment, Chuddy enters the room. He and Robbie share a nod and I beam with joy.

Chuddy beams too, "Good morning everyone, what a nice photo that's going to be."

Robbie responded, "It will be even better if you jump in the middle next to Ms. Gisele." Chuddy complies with her suggestion and takes hold of my hand. She continued, "On the count of three, everyone say cheese."

She neglected to tell the students where to look at the end of the count, half look at me and the other half look at her. Chuddy whispers, "This photo is epic, it's a keeper."

I whispered right back, "So are you." Then I loudly announced that it was story time. "Who wants to share their photographs and story this week?"

After class, Chuddy agrees to join me, Sophia and her mother as we search for a new puppy.

Later that day, Dad is suited up as usual and wears coordinating thick-framed bifocals. He crouches behind shrubbery across the street from an Oakland Biker Club, and aims a long-lens camera at the doorway.

A young woman exits the club. She appears weathered and older than her twenty years, sports tattoos on her neck and wears lip and nose rings. She has a partially shaved head and is dressed in leather biker gear. Dad snaps several photographs of her before she puts on a helmet, jumps onto a motorcycle and rides off.

✦ ✦ ✦ ✦ ✦

CPSIA information can be obtained
at www.ICGtesting.com
Printed in the USA
FSHW022314171021
85538FS